MURDER ANY WITCH WAY

BRIMSTONE BAY MYSTERIES - BOOK 1

N.M. HOWELL

DUNGEON MEDIA CORP.

CHAPTER ONE

MY HEART RACED, THE BEADS OF SWEAT DRIPPING down my forehead stinging my eyes. I was thankful for the ocean spray that cooled my skin under the late summer sun.

Politics… has anyone done anything scandalous lately? It's small town Maine. Of course, not.

"… And then he showed up wearing these little tight teal pants, prancing around like he owned the place. I mean really, teal? That's so last season."

I had almost forgotten Riley and I were still on a call. My chest ached, but I pushed on. I tried to make a point of going running at least once a day. If nothing else, it helped me wind down after a stressful day at work. It was much nicer running around the boardwalk near the ocean than in the city streets, and it was a great excuse to get fresh air and to clear my head. I did my best thinking when I ran.

"… And to top it all off, he wore an avocado green hat. Avocado green! I mean seriously, what was he trying to prove combining those colors?"

What about the economy? I wonder if there's anything sinister happening at the local treasury. That would make a good piece for the paper.

"River? Earth to River. Are you even listening to me?" Riley's voice groaned in my ear. "Honestly, girl, all that salty sea air is getting to your head."

"Huh? Yea, sorry." Breathless, I pulled my thoughts back to our conversation. What had we been talking about? It took a moment to focus back on Riley's words. "Right, I'm listening. Teal and green…"

I pushed forward, intent on maintaining my pace through Riley's chatter. The rising sun glared in my eyes, and I had to squint to see ahead of me. It was well into September, and I was determined to enjoy the warm weather while I had the chance before the dreary gray fall set in. It was still morning, and the sun was casting long shadows on the ground as I passed around the windy boardwalk that clung to the edge of the rocky bay behind where I lived.

Riley continued his story despite my distraction. "And he didn't even pay me a second glance. I might as well have been a shadow…"

I glanced down at my shadow as I ran.

… shadow.

I halted in my tracks, nearly toppling over my

own feet. Folding over to use my knees as supports, I struggled to regain my breath. "That's it! I've got it. Okay, Riley, I gotta go."

I pressed the little button to click off my headpiece before Riley had a chance to protest. I was going to pay for that later, but I had bigger things on my mind. He had been with me all through my studies in New York, he knew how demanding any journalism job was. He would forgive me. Eventually. With a grin on my face, I picked up the pace again and veered off from the boardwalk to head back home to shower quickly before going to work. This was why I ran. My best ideas always come to me while running, and this town certainly had enough space for it.

I wouldn't say Brimstone Bay was exactly the most exciting place to live, but the town itself and its seaside landscape were undoubtedly beautiful. As a witch, living in a small town definitely wasn't ideal. At least, in the big cities, we didn't have to hide as much. There were underground nightclubs where we could be ourselves. The kind of places that you could go to hang out with others of your kind, no masks no magical veils. But small towns, so I've found, tended to be highly superstitious. They were a different story, entirely. Many people across the United States still swore that witchcraft came solely from fairy tales, but for those who were aware, it was often a highly-contested subject. People were either fascinated by us, or desperate to become our friends, learn our tricks, and witness our magic. Others, on the other hand, were downright terrified of us and would burn us at the stake had they the chance. Back in New York, while I never flaunted my magic, I at least had a decent support group with others of my kind. Since moving to Brimstone Bay, I really needed to be more careful about hiding my true self.

I was lucky to find this place, though, as I had no idea where I would end up after graduating from NYU with my journalism degree. I knew I would never get a job right away in any big city, interns never did. I had to make a name for myself first as every young journalist does. Only then could I return home and advance my career.

I slowed down as I approached the street that marked my new home. Number twenty-one Black Cat Lane. I couldn't help but laugh at the irony of it every time I passed the street sign. Of course, the witch would live on a street called Black Cat Lane. It was entirely coincidental, I swear. At least, I believed it to be.

After my graduation, I spent a lot of time looking for jobs around the United States. There was a brand-new local newspaper opening its doors in Brimstone Bay that was willing to hire inexperienced journalists, and there happened to be a shared house with a spare room available that I found on an online witch forum—online forums only available to the paranormal community—requiring magic, of course, to access the sites.

At number twenty-one stood a beautiful Victorian seaside mansion, complete with turret, bay windows, wraparound veranda, and creaky stairs. The 1859 house was stunning but looked like it hadn't been maintained in over a century. The purple and ivory paint flaked, and some of the trim boards were falling apart, likely because the owner was nearly as old as the house. I had offered to help her fix it up a bit when I first moved in, but Mrs. Brody brushed it off with mutterings of 'it's not necessary' and 'it's fine the way it is.' The house stood grand and proud, but just derelict enough not to garner any unwanted attention. Set back far from the street, we were offered enough privacy from onlookers that we didn't need to be afraid of showing our magic freely while at home. The best part? I lived with three other twenty-something-year-old witches.

The sun finally rose above the rooftops, and the rest of my housemates would likely be waking up soon. I stretched as I walked toward the back of the house to use the rear doorway, hoping that I would be able to sneak in and prevent having to chat with anyone before rushing to work. I didn't have time to deal with any distractions. I needed to get into the office while the ideas were fresh in my head.

"Hi, Mrs. Brody," I said as I passed our ancient,

pint-size landlady who busied about in her basement apartment on the other side of the large window. She casually waved her hand at me without looking up, apparently preoccupied with whatever she worked on inside. I quietly opened the back door and tiptoed up the stairs to the bathroom to have a quick shower. As I was towel-drying my hair after getting dressed, I could hear footsteps coming from the floor above me, and I quickly threw the towel on the floor, grabbed my jacket, and slipped back down the stairs and out of the house before being seen by any of my housemates. I adored my housemates dearly, but I had no time for chit-chat. There was work to be done.

I grabbed my bike, slung my backpack over my shoulder, and took off toward the main street of our sleepy little town to catch my boss as early as I could before she got busy with any of the other new journalists.

The warm morning air dried my hair as I rode, resulting in a tousled mess of chocolate-brown knots when I arrived. Not that I much cared. Mascara and lip balm were the daily extents of my makeup routine, to the dismay of the girls I lived with. More concerned about being taken seriously than fawned over for my looks, my sun-dried tangled hair and messily applied mascara was my go-to look for the day.

Downtown Brimstone Bay was beautiful. Shops,

restaurants, antique stores and bookshops lined the main street and plenty of green space to hang around in outside sprawled among the buildings. On rare sunny days, you couldn't find a spot in the gardens if you tried.

The Brimstone Press sat conveniently above a small café, which suited me just fine as being a journalist and a coffee addict seemed to go hand-in-hand. I poked my head through the café door and shouted my regular order to Ryan, who was busy in the back room. "Be right down in two minutes to grab it!"

The door to our office was locked, and I had to dig through my bag to find the key. I fumbled with the lock before racing up the stairs to our tiny workspace to do some digging through our filing cabinet before JoAnn, my editor, arrived.

I must've spent a long time digging through the drawers because there was a knock at the office door and Ryan came walking in with my triple Americano, extra hot, black. Just how I liked it. He smiled and set it down on my desk and leaned against the door casually as he watched me rummage through the files that I had strewn across the floor.

"Thanks, Ryan," I said without turning my head. Determined to find what I needed before JoAnn arrived, my fingers furiously sorted through the cabinet. When setting my mind to a task, it was hard to pull me away. Call me obsessive if you will, but I like to think of it as focused. Okay, maybe a tiny bit obsessive.

"Sure," he said to me. "What are you up to later?"

I really didn't have time for casual conversation. Couldn't he tell I was busy? "Girls night at home," I lied.

"You know, there are a ton of really great apartments available for rent nearby," he said conversationally. "If you want to get away from the whole roommate thing, I mean."

"Uh-huh." I continued to look through the papers in front of me. Ryan had been trying to convince me to move out of the house since I first moved to Brimstone Bay. I got the impression that he didn't like the girls very much. Either that, or he was hoping for a private place to invite himself over to. I wasn't all that great at reading guys, having been relationship-challenged my whole life.

He finally caught on that I wasn't interested in chatting. "Ok, then. Well… See you later?"

"Yep."

Sighing, Ryan turned and left, shutting the door quietly behind him. Voices echoed up through the stairs, and I guessed JoAnn had finally arrived. I did my best to quickly gather all the papers up off the floor and tossed them in a messy pile on my desk just as my editor walked in with two hot coffees in hand.

"Ah, you've already got a coffee." JoAnn yawned as she shuffled to my desk.

"It's a two-coffee kind of morning." I eagerly reached for the extra coffee she had in her hand.

Her eyes narrowed once she settled at her desk. "Today will be a busy day. Just a heads up. We've got a lot of work to do and not much time to do it. I need you to be on your A-game today."

Every day was a busy day at the office, given that the paper had only been around for a few weeks and we were still trying to make a name for ourselves. JoAnn worked us extra hard, often expecting ten stories from each of us at a time, just to be sure that we didn't run out of fresh material for the paper. It was a weekly publication, but by the number of hours that we worked every day, you would think that it was a daily report. I rolled my eyes with my back to her and took a big swig of the burning-hot coffee. I felt immediately revived.

When I turned back to face her, I noticed her eyeing the messy stack of papers I had on my desk. Her brow lifted quizzically as it often did when she is looking for an answer.

"Oh, I just had an idea for a story," I replied to her unanswered question. "I wanted to get in early and prepare before you got here, but I'm not too sure I found what I was looking for."

"Okay then, let's hear it." JoAnn picked up her cup, leaned back in her reclining chair with her feet up on the desk, and took a long sip of coffee. "What've you got?"

"Well, I was thinking. Nothing too exciting ever really seems to happen in this sleepy town. Why don't we make something happen?"

She looked skeptical. "I'm listening."

"Well." I chose my words cautiously. "I heard the Shadow Festival is passing through Portland this week. Why don't we ask them if they'll come through Brimstone Bay on their tour?"

I sat in my chair and sipped my coffee, watching JoAnn as she stared at me wide-eyed. She laughed suddenly. "You actually think a town like Brimstone Bay would allow the Shadow Festival to come through?" She laughed again.

"No, think about it. Summer is almost over, and before we know it, fall will be here. The Shadow Festival will get people excited for the Halloween season. If anything, it will bring money into the town and help all the local businesses. Besides, who doesn't love a little spooky fun?"

She continued to laugh and shake her head. "It's just not going to happen."

"It would make for a great story," I said. "There are only so many births, birthdays, and deaths that we can put in the paper before people start dying of boredom from what we're writing."

Her expression flared at my words, and I knew I had stepped over the line. I knew we were building a readership and that it would take time for the paper to really find its identity. I knew the stories would come, but it didn't change the fact that our front page last week featured the town's new street cleaning machine. After a long pause, JoAnn finally spoke. "I agree, it would make for a great story. It would certainly liven up this sleepy town. But there's no way to get anyone here to agree to let the festival come through, you know the kind of people who live here. The ones who are vocal." JoAnn sat her cup on her desk and opened her laptop to begin her day's work.

I chewed my lip, trying to think of ways that we could get past this hurdle. The Shadow Festival was a traveling fair that went from the West Coast to the East Coast and back again each year, celebrating all things paranormal. Most people assumed it was just a show and took their kids there as a fun way to celebrate the beginning of the Halloween season. But most didn't know its true purpose. The faire was an excuse to draw the paranormal community together, allowing us to expose our true selves to some degree among paranormals and normal people alike. I had been three times over the years, two of which were with Riley who had no idea that the werewolf he had been flirting with had actually been a wolf. Everyone loved it. They had all the typical treats like candied apples and caramel corn, but the real treat was seeing all the witches, werewolves, ghouls, and other paranormal creatures coming out in their full glory. They could be out and about and wouldn't have to hide behind closed doors. The concept was liberating.

Of course, most people just figured they wore costumes and acted as part of the show, but everyone from within the paranormal community knew otherwise. It was a fun way for us to get together, celebrate our heritage, and finally get to be ourselves in front of non-magical people. Not only fun and exciting, the festival always drew a massive crowd and brought a lot of money into each city it traveled through. It was just the kind of thing that Brimstone Bay needed, both socially and economically.

"Well, if I can find a way to get approval from the mayor…" I eyed JoAnn eagerly.

She glanced up at me from behind her laptop, raised her eyebrow again and made a *mmhmm* sound. "Well, you have my blessing, River. Good luck with that."

I grinned. What JoAnn didn't know was that our young new mayor had a bit of a crush on me, and I had a feeling that I could persuade him to allow the festival to come through town. He had also conveniently spent the better part of twenty years living in Los Angeles and was familiar with the paranormal community. At least to some extent. Mayor Scott confided in me that he had a number of friends that were witches back in the city. While I never admitted to being one myself, I suspected he had a hunch.

I gulped down my first coffee, grabbed the second, picked up my sweater and backpack, and bounded out the front door before JoAnn said a word.

CHAPTER TWO

With coffee in hand, I walked down the cobblestone main street of town towards Mayor Scott's office. As much as I complained about my job, I really enjoyed the normalcy of many of the tasks. It was nice not worrying about witch stuff all the time, and just enjoying the simple pleasures of being a girl. Don't get me wrong, I absolutely loved being a witch and had mad respect for my heritage, but sometimes it was just nice being normal. Pretending to be, anyway.

I came from a long line of witches, the Halloway Clan, and spent my earlier years with my dad and his family in Long Island City, New York. Everyone in the family was either a witch or was married to a witch or some other paranormal being. Our house was filled with magic daily. Flying coffee cups and magical pranks were the norm in my house; that was until my dad died in a freak accident at work. I moved to Manhattan not long after the accident to get away from my family. The constant reminder of my dad was too painful for me to handle. I needed a break.

That was when I enrolled in the journalism program at NYU. The University had a paranormal club, which I occasionally visited just to fill the magical void I felt being away from my family for so long. I would also go out with some of the other club members to a few of the underground witch bars scattered around the city, but for the most part, I just focused on my studies.

In Brimstone Bay, my housemates and Mrs. Brody were my family. The house was always filled with magic, making it feel like my home back in New York. I got on well with the other girls in the house and truly enjoyed living there. None of them really had jobs, though, and it was difficult making them understand that I needed to spend a great deal of my time doing research and writing articles. Sometimes it was nice to just get out of the house and focus on my own work without the distraction of four witches. Apart from that, though, I enjoyed spending time at home.

There weren't many alternatives for friends in this town, anyway. Most people blew off the idea of witchcraft as if it were some tale designed to scare children. Then there were the ones who believed it but were downright terrified of being turned into toads - which, of course, was ridiculous. Well, sort of. And then there were the very few who believed everything that they've heard on TV about witches to be true and obsessed with becoming friends with one. It was for those reasons that I never knew what to expect when I went anywhere public. I was either greeted politely, with complete disdain, or sheer adoration. None of us had admitted to anyone outside of the house that we were witches, so the town people's attitude towards us was based on pure speculation.

We all, of course, had our close friends who knew the truth. We didn't have to hide who we were when they came to stay, but unfortunately, none of them actually lived in town. I only got to see any of my good friends when they came to visit from New York, which, of course, was very rare. Riley, for example, had only come to visit once when I first moved, preferring the flamboyant excitement of the big city to the "dreary dullness" of the small town, as he put it. If Brimstone Bay wasn't accepting of witches, they certainly would not be accepting of a gay male witch.

I suspected JoAnn knew I was a witch. She was exceptionally smart and spent many years traveling the world. One doesn't spend that much time in new cultures without gaining at least some knowledge or appreciation of the paranormal. Magic is far less discreet in the more liberal cities around the world. Considering the way she studied me when I arrived on the first day of my job, I had a hunch she knew straight away what I was, though nothing was ever said. Mayor Scott, on the other hand, was less discreet about his assumptions, often making not-so-subtle magical puns whenever I was around him. I kept my mouth shut like any good witch should. He still liked to tease me about it, and I let him because, well, with a face like that, I'd let him get away with just about anything.

"Morning River, what's news?" He smiled up at me from his large wooden desk as I entered his office. He always greeted me with the same line, obviously thinking himself clever.

"Oh you know, the usual," I flirted. "Another bouncing baby boy born, another 90th birthday…" I trailed off, noticing the thousands of posters scattered over his desk and on the floor. His two young assistants were desperately trying to sort through stacks of announcement print-outs and posters with the words "Shadow Festival" printed across the pages. They must have blown all over the office due to the wind that blew in through the door. The mayor insisted on always keeping it open. It made him seem welcoming or something along those lines.

"What's news with you?" I asked, amused at the carnage that was taking place in his office. I leaned against the door frame, sipping my coffee and watching the scene unfold in front of me. I couldn't help the smile that spread across my lips as I re-read the words on the posters.

Mayor Scott leaned back in his chair, put his feet up on his desk, and gestured his muscled arms across the room dramatically.

"How did you manage to get town approval for this one?" I asked in awe. "I don't remember this ever coming up during the town meeting."

Mayor Connor Scott laughed a deep, cheerful laugh. "Ah, this town needs a little excitement. At this point, I would rather deal with the letters of complaint after the event is over than have to deal with the drama that ensues at every town hall meeting whenever a new idea is brought forward. I've had it up to here with those bloody church groups and lonely old widows clubs who always knock any progressive idea to the floor before anyone even has a chance to consider it in this town. The stress of it is too much, and I can't afford to lose any of this hair." He ran his fingers through this tousled dark locks that hung loosely over his eyes. He had a habit of brushing his hair away from his face, and he knew the effect it had on women. The only reason a place like Brimstone Bay allowed a guy like him to be elected mayor was that he came from a family with old money who had lived in town for the past few hundred years. The name Scott was scattered around many downtown buildings, and people generally had a lot of respect for the name.

I smirked. "Well, your hair looks fine. And I'm going to pretend I didn't hear that other part." He smiled up at me with those big, bright green eyes of his. I did my best not to swoon like a giddy schoolgirl. I think I managed it. Think being the operative word, there.

"Do you need any help?" I asked, forcing myself to break eye contact.

"No thanks, we've got it. Right, ladies?" His two assistants ignored him, obviously annoyed with their task.

"I'll leave you to it then." I turned to leave but glanced back one last time. "When is the festival coming through?" I tried my best to sound casual to not give away my excitement.

"The first week of October," he said. He got up and walked over to me, handing me the stack of mini posters. "Here, take these back to JoAnn. If anything, you should have some juicy stories about how enraged the town will become at its new, unpredictable mayor." He winked.

I took the stack and left, waving casually over my shoulder as I walked away down the sidewalk.

Yeesh, that man was good-looking. Why he chose to come back to Brimstone Bay and work in politics is beyond me. He could have built a successful career in LA as an actor or something.

Ah, well. Lucky for us girls, we at least had something nice to look at other than the architecture.

It didn't take long for me to get back to the Brimstone Press.

"You're kidding me," JoAnn said incredulously as I walked up the stairs to our office with the stack of posters. "How the hell did you manage that?"

I laughed. She rarely swore, and I knew she must have been impressed because the word hell was way out of character for her.

I shrugged. "I guess good ideas travel fast."

"When?" she asked, tossing a few papers aside to clear room on her desk for her calendar. JoAnn was funny - she embraced new technologies, always eager to test out the latest gadgets. In business matters, though, she always relied on her hand-written notes and a printed calendar with kittens on it.

"First week of October," I answered. I tucked one of the posters in my bag and placed the rest on the corner of her desk.

"Ok great, that gives us lots of time to prep," she replied with a grin, clearly pleased. "We'll want to write a piece announcing the festival, of course, and then some background stories leading up to it." I nodded along, grabbing my notebook and pen so I could jot down notes as she spoke.

"We will obviously want to cover all aspects of the event as it unfolds, both the event itself and the town's response to it," she continued. "And definitely a few follow-up pieces, discussing the long-term, hopefully positive, effects the event will have on the town. With any luck, if we spin this the right way, this might result in Brimstone Bay opening up a little bit to future events."

I nodded, writing furiously as she spoke.

"I'd like you to write the first piece today," she said.

I looked up at her, wide-eyed. "Me?" I asked. "Don't you want to write that one yourself?"

She shook her head. "No, I think this is a great opportunity for you to build your portfolio and discover your voice." I was flattered until it dawned on me that she most likely didn't want her name attached to any story relating to the controversial event.

I chewed my lip. Well, if the town wasn't weary of me yet, they certainly would be after that. Ah well, great exposure, I supposed.

"I won't let you down," I said cheerily, packing up my bag with a few necessary items to complete my research. I would have to go home, grab my good laptop to do some research, and then maybe go around interviewing a few people about the event. I would have to select them carefully so as not to end up with a bunch of cranky and threatening quotes for the article.

"Oh, and River," JoAnn continued as I headed

for the door. "I'd like you to cover Mr. Johnston's 95th birthday party tonight. It's at the hall on 4th."

I groaned and rolled my eyes.

"Will do!" I bounded for the door before she could pawn any more boring stories off on me. Let the other guys handle those, for a change.

The sun was bright, and it was another lovely late summer's day. I strolled slowly through town on my way home, choosing to walk my bike instead of riding straight home.

I noticed the smell of warm spices emanating from Mrs. Pots' Bakery as I walked by, and couldn't resist the urge to go in to see what she was cooking up.

Mrs. Pots was a lovely, portly little woman with a kind smile that could warm even the coldest of hearts. She was the closest thing in town that we witches had to a friend. Apart from the mayor, of course. I often stopped by to chat on my way to and from work. She always welcomed us warmly every time one of us stopped by, always eager to tell us about her latest encounter.

Mrs. Pots claimed she could speak to ghosts, you see. As I never knew any non-witch to be able to even see ghosts, I highly doubted her stories. A witch could normally tell when he or she was in the company of another magical being, and Mrs. Pots gave no hint of having any magical aura whatsoever. That being said, she was adamant that she could, in fact, speak with the otherworldly, so who was I to say otherwise?

As I walked in, she was busying herself in front of the ovens, frantically pulling out cookie sheets filled to the brim with miniature pies and quickly replacing them with new ones as the baked goods came out perfectly golden brown.

"Smells amazing, Mrs. Pots," I said as I walked in the door. She hadn't noticed me come in, and she jumped in surprise when my voice startled her.

"Oh, it's you, dear." She smiled sweetly and wiped her hands on her apron as she closed the oven door on another batch of miniature pies. "Lovely to see you, sweetheart. How is work going?"

"Wonderful," I said, her cheery attitude was always contagious. She came around the counter to give me a big squeeze of a hug. I loved Mrs. Pots like family, and she certainly filled the maternal void as best as anyone could. Mrs. Brody took good care of us girls at the house, but she was the furthest thing from maternal anyone could get.

Mrs. Pots handed me a cookie from the counter, always trying her best to fatten me up.

"The Shadow Festival is coming to town," I said through a mouthful of butter cookie, crumbs falling down all over my shirt.

"Are you serious?" she asked, beaming up at me. She jumped up and down with joy like a little girl, clapping her hands together in delight. "Oh, how wonderful! Just think of the spirits I will get to meet. What an absolute delight. I must text my nephew, he won't want to miss this." She pulled her pink-cased phone from her apron pocket and immediately set to texting. Her plump fingers flew wildly across the screen.

I had met her nephew Roger when I first moved to town. He was a clever kid and had an absolute obsession with witches. I'm not sure what Mrs. Pots had told him, but he followed me around like a lap dog for three full days, before heading back home to Vermont. I shouldn't really call him a kid, as he was only a handful of years younger than I was. But at 19 he was still a teenager, which made him a kid to me.

"He would be delighted to help you with your stories, I'm sure."

I did my best to look polite as she beamed up at me, but honestly, that was the last thing I wanted right now. I had enough work to do as it was, and I didn't need a shadow following me around everywhere. "Oh, I doubt he'll enjoy that," I offered. "It's boring work being a journalist."

"Oh nonsense," she replied, smiling down at her buzzing phone. By her absolutely thrilled facial expression, I imagined Roger was equally as excited as she was. Yipee.

I smiled at her, trying to direct the conversation away from her nephew before I had to commit to anything else. "It will be interesting to see how the town responds to the news," I said. "I'm supposed to write an article announcing the event. Would you be interested in offering a quote I can use for the paper? It would be nice to get some positive perspective on it."

Before she could answer, the door chimed behind me. Bailey bounded in, panting and out of breath.

Bailey was one of my housemates, and she always seemed to be in a rush.

"Hey," I said to her through another crumbly mouthful of cookie. She nodded up at me in acknowledgment, bent over nearly half-way, leaning against her legs for support.

"Get chased here by a bear?" I laughed at her.

She shook her head. "Mrs. Brody…needs…her pies," she said, through forced breath.

I raised my eyebrow at her. "What on earth does Mrs. Brody need all those pies for?" I eyed the counter. It was covered end to end in at least a few dozen mini pies.

Bailey finally caught her breath and wiped a sweaty strand of blond hair from her face. "She's having another bridge night and wants to impress her guests."

I rolled my eyes. Mrs. Brody has bridge nights nearly every week, but based on her recent events, I didn't think her guests were likely to be interested in pies.

"They're nearly ready, dear," Mrs. Pots said, bustling about behind the counter. "Another ten minutes and they'll be ready to go."

"What's that spice I smell?" I sniffed the air. It smelled so familiar.

"Cloves, dear," Mrs. Pots said, her voice muffled as she poked her nose into the warm oven behind the counter.

"Ah." My dad used to brew tea at home with cloves; that's why it smelled so familiar. I breathed in the warm scent, the memories flooding back. "How creative," I said finally.

"Well, I've had to step up my game since Mr. Hoity-Toity Bramley and his blabbering son Ryan started carrying those imported cakes in the café."

Bailey blushed and preoccupied herself with rubbing out a scuff mark on the bakery floor with her sandal. Bailey often hung around the café, having had a crush on Ryan for the past few years, or so the other girls told me. Her long blond hair and slim curves had guys drooling over her everywhere she went. She could have any guy in town, but she had her sights set on geeky Ryan Bramley, yet was far too shy to do anything about it. All the girls in the house knew, of course. It was often discussed that we should cast a spell of encouragement on the poor guy so he would build up his confidence enough to ask her out himself. Spells like that are dangerous, though, and we didn't want to screw anything up for Bailey if we could help it. Besides, we vowed that we would never use magic on anyone outside of the house. House rules, and all that.

Mrs. Pots took the last of the hot pies out of the oven and placed them carefully in the pretty pink containers her shop was known for, muttering something about "stupid city cakes".

We helped Mrs. Pots pack up the pies in the tidy little containers and placed them in cardboard boxes for easier transport.

"Help me carry these home?" Bailey asked, picking up one of the boxes and carrying it high to hide her glowing cheeks.

"Sure," I laughed. I was still unsure what the purpose of the pies was.

Mrs. Brody's bridge nights consisted of her and the local ghosts. Often at least a dozen or so of them would show up, and they all sat around the table chatting. There was no bridge to be played, of course, as ghosts were unable to handle material objects. They were unable to eat, too, but I kept my mouth shut.

I eyed Bailey questioningly, but she just shrugged. We never truly understood what went on in Mrs. Brody's mind, but we learned to stop asking questions we didn't want to know the answers to.

Mrs. Pots placed a small container of sugar cookies on top of the pile in my cardboard box, insisting we share them with the other girls.

"You're going to make us all fat, Mrs. Pots," Bailey said as she held the door open for me.

"That's the plan, girls, that's the plan." She waved goodbye to us. "Come back soon."

We left, and I struggled to balance the massive box of pies on my bike seat as we made our way back home to deliver Mrs. Brody's pies. The delicious smell from the boxes garnered a few sidelong glances from passersby as we made our way down the winding streets of the town.

If anything, at least it looked like we were preparing for a social event. Since we were rarely seen with anyone besides each other, I hoped it would make us at least appear to be somewhat normal.

"One last thing," Bailey said to me, eyeing me sideways.

"What's that?" I didn't dare take my eyes off the box of pies balancing dangerously on my bike.

"Mrs. Brody has invited us to bridge night."

CHAPTER THREE

AFTER DELIVERING THE PIES TO MRS. BRODY IN THE basement apartment, Bailey and I joined the girls upstairs for some down time before I had to race off to cover Mr. Thompson's birthday party. At least at 95 years of age, your energy levels are low, and the party wasn't likely to last very long. I would show up, snap a few photos, get a quote from the birthday boy, and be on my way.

As I got upstairs, Rory was busy preening in front of the large ornate mirror on the third floor. That girl spent more time fussing with her face than she did sleeping. Despite her vain outward appearance, though, she was a really down-to-earth person. She was always the one I went to when I had to vent about my day at work.

Jane was the exact opposite. Sporty and outgoing, she was always the life of the party.

"Hey girl," Jane called out to me, as I climbed the rickety staircase to the third floor where she and Rory's rooms were. There was a large open lounge room with windows along the entire back wall that overlooked the bay on their floor, so we often hung out up here. Jane was lying back on the couch, her feet kicked up over one of the armrests.

"Hey," I said, squeezing onto the couch next to her. "What are you guys up to?"

"We've been invited to Mrs. Brody's super-secret bridge night in four hours if you haven't heard," she said. "So naturally, Rory needs to start preparing."

Rory threw a makeup brush at her, narrowly missing Jane's head by an inch and landing by Bailey's feet as she came up the stairs.

The makeup brush magically flew back through the room, landing on Rory's makeup table.

"Thanks," she said to Bailey, without taking her eyes away from the serious business of applying fake eyelashes.

Bailey was a very talented witch and often didn't even have to lift a finger or utter an incantation to cast a spell. We were all secretly jealous of her, but no one would admit it.

We spent the hour chatting about life and men and other such things. Before long, I checked my watch and grudgingly headed back down to my room to get my tape recorder and notebook so I could go and cover Mr. Thompson's damned party.

"I'll see you guys later," I called back as I made my way carefully down the stairs. Not only was the staircase creaky, but it was exceptionally narrow, and if you didn't watch where you put your feet, it was easy to miss a step and fall crashing down to the next floor. Trust me, it's happened more than once over the past few weeks - and it wasn't even after I had been drinking.

Mr. Thompson's party was just as I expected it to be: a bunch of old people, some sort of tapioca pudding instead of cake, and a few screaming great-grandchildren running around the floor. Tripping hazards, if you asked me. I smiled warmly at the group, wished the man Happy Birthday, snapped a few photos and asked him to say a few words for the paper. He grunted into the microphone, obviously not pleased that he was forced to sit through such an ordeal. I gave up on the quote, bid him farewell, and was on my way.

Quick and painless, and I could check this one off the list.

I hurried back to the house so I could type up the article quickly, and then hopefully make some headway on the Shadow Festival announcement before heading down to Mrs. Brody's place for bridge night. I had no idea what to expect, but by the dulcet tones of my housemates, I wasn't expecting it to be a very lively time.

It was already four o'clock when I got home, so I typed fast and worked quickly, managing to get a good chunk of my work done before the girls came down to get me.

"Ready for the *party*?" Jane mused, emphasizing the word 'party' as she came into my room. Rory shushed her dramatically. The house was large, but the walls were thin, and sound traveled fast in this old place.

"As ready as I'll ever be," I laughed, closing my laptop and stuffing my notes and recorder back in my bag.

We followed the smell of spiced pie down to Mrs. Brody's apartment and knocked on the door.

She shouted "come in" from behind the door, and we let ourselves into the tiny basement apartment.

I don't know what I was expecting, but it wasn't this.

The apartment was filled with smoke that came pouring out from the kitchen. Mrs. Brody obviously had been cooking, and I could see large cauldrons of something boiling away on her stove-top. I could also see a small steaming pot of something else that smelled suspiciously of devil's root herb, but I knew better than to ask. I had a particularly good nose for herbs. I would often spend hours on end with my dad in our kitchen as a kid, concocting up all sorts of creative spells and potions. I didn't say anything, and no one else seemed to notice. She was a seasoned witch, and she knew what she was doing.

Peering through the smoke, I could barely make out the forms of a large group of men sitting around the massive wooden table in the living room. I never had an affinity for spirits, and they often appeared light and wispy to me. It was hard to make them out from the cooking smoke.

Mrs. Brody has been entertaining these men for years, and obviously had grown accustomed to having the presence of ghosts in her house. I wasn't used to it at all, as you rarely encountered spirits in big cities. I don't know if it was the bustling energy or crowded population, but I don't think I even saw one ghost while living in New York City.

I stared at them, unsure what to do or say. Rory smirked at me and walked confidently into the room. She took a seat next to the form of a man wearing a tightly-buttoned jacket and top hat and struck up a conversation as if they were the best of friends. Rory had been in the house the longest, so for all I knew, they were.

Mrs. Brody came scurrying out of the kitchen and ushered us to our seats at the table.

"Sit, sit, girls," she said frantically. "I'll bring out your meals in a second."

Mrs. Brody was good that way, often preparing

home-cooked meals for us on a nightly basis. If it weren't for her, I would be living off frozen dinners and Ramen noodles. I offered to help her serve, but she insisted I stay put with her guests.

While we waited for her to bring out the food, I listened intently on the conversation that was going on amongst the ghostly forms across the table.

"Have you heard?" one said, with a deep southern drawl. "The Shadow Festival is coming to town."

"How absurd," another replied. "Who would attend such a thing?"

"A festival dedicated to the paranormal," the first continued. "What a ridiculous idea."

"Absolutely preposterous," another said from the other end of the table. "Who would dedicate the time to such an absolutely ridiculous theme."

I tried to suppress a laugh. It was hilarious listening to a group of paranormal beings discuss the absurdity of a paranormal festival. I didn't have the heart to say that they fit directly into the demographic of the event. I kept quiet, listening intently to the men bicker back and forth about the preposterous festival.

Mrs. Brody brought out massive bowls of delicious smelling stew, placing them in front of the four of us. She sat down at the table without one for herself and began chatting with the ghost of the old man next to her.

I found it strange that there were no female ghosts, but given Mrs. Brody's abrasive personality towards outsiders, I had a feeling she wasn't one to have many close girlfriends.

The stew smelled delicious, but I felt weird eating in front of a group of spirits who were unable to eat anything themselves. The other girls obviously felt the same awkwardness, as nobody touched their food.

"Oh, go on. Eat, eat." Mrs. Brody insisted, waving her hands frantically in front of her. "Don't mind this lot, they haven't been hungry in years."

Awkward.

I sighed and resigned to eating the stew, doing my best to ignore the looks from the spirits around me. Through my peripherals, I could barely make them out from the smoke anyway. And after a few minutes of looking, I realized how starved I was, and inhaled the rest of the meal.

The awkwardness slowly subsided as the evening went on. Our bowls were cleared away, and replaced with playing cards and pies, which I was confident were just there for decoration.

We all listened as Mrs. Brodie bickered with her friends. For men who appeared to have lived over a hundred years ago, some of them have quite progressive opinions.

"I recently heard that Rivertown has a new female mayor!" The man with the top hat exclaimed.

"A female mayor?" another asked. "Preposterous!"

"Oh, don't be such an old prude, Barry," said another.

"Yes, and not only is she female," the top hat-wearing spirit continued, "but I hear she is married to a woman, and they have a child together!"

"About time women took over in politics, I say," the form of a small man in a bow tie announced. "How wonderful."

"A woman marrying a woman? How ridiculous!" another proclaimed. "How on earth do they even have a child together? That makes no sense. It's ridiculous, I say."

"Use your imagination, man," another said jovially. "My word, what a delight. How fresh and exciting these times are."

"I hear lesbians are popping up all over the country," another said.

"Ah yes, it's quite trendy these days."

"Absolutely preposterous."

I rolled my eyes. Men.

The evening continued with more conversation, and I even joined in after a while. One of the men was quite interested in my work, as Brimstone Bay has never had a local paper before. We discussed a few of the stories I had written, and I explained how nothing ever exciting really happened in town, and as a result, the paper was more of a weekly log of births, birthdays, and deaths.

"It was not always so," one man said to me, as he stood up before his friends. The room hushed. "Brimstone Bay was once a dark place. A dreaded place." His voice took on a haunted tone. "Back in my day, the town was wrought with murder and scandal," he continued, waving his hand in the air for dramatic effect.

"No way," I said. "I've never encountered anything to support that in any of my research." I crossed my arms and leaned back in my chair, eager to hear what he had to say. He scowled at me, obviously not impressed that I interrupted his story.

"Ah, my dear," he continued. "Don't believe everything you read. The youth today are so quick to believe."

I glanced around the room, but to my surprise all the other men were nodding along, seemingly agreeing with his story.

"Okay, go on then," I said. "I'm interested."

The spirit cleared his throat. "Do you not know how men become ghosts?" He paused for dramatic effect. "To remain on this cruel earth as a spirit, one's life must have ended either by murder or suicide."

"So, wait," Jane said, reaching for one of the pies. "You were all murdered?"

Mrs. Brody quickly slapped Jane's hand away

from the pie. "That's' not for you, dear." We all eyed the woman suspiciously but knew better than to pry.

Ignoring Mrs. Brody's quiet outburst, they all nodded at Jane, except for one.

"Yes, girl, and all within this town," one said. "Well, all except for Jerry, there." He motioned towards the small man at the end of the table.

"Well, you would have jumped in front of a train too, if you had been married to Buella," he groaned. The spirits all laughed, relishing in the memories.

I stared open-mouthed, unsure how to respond.

"Why doesn't anyone know about this? Why isn't any of this recorded in the library?" I asked.

"Oh, my dear," the spirit continued. "It's one of the biggest cover-ups of our age."

Another spirit spoke up. "After years of darkness and murder, the town became populated with spirits. It became a mecca for the paranormal, and that was simply not acceptable for the rest of the community. Witches were burned at the stake, and the spirits were driven out."

The first man continued, "It took years of burning records and rewriting history. For all everyone knows now, Brimstone Bay is a quiet, unassuming little town. It's absurd, but there's obviously nothing we can do about it." He rolled his eyes, and the others nodded in agreement.

"Where do you think the town gets its name from?" another asked, looking at us expectantly.

We all shook our heads. "It's been named that for hundreds of years, has it not?" I asked.

"No, my dear. This town was once known as Birchwood, and it wasn't until after the Puritans rose up and slaughtered the witches and banished the spirits that it was renamed Brimstone Bay. It's in reference to the Bible, of course. The wrath of God."

"The wrath of the damned Puritans," another man said. I looked at him and noticed he was dressed in a high-collared jacket and distinctly large black hat. The other men chuckled at him.

"Were you one of them?" I asked, recognizing his clothing from movies I've seen on similar subjects.

"Aye, I was," he responded somberly, "but I do not agree with what they did during those years. Murder, it was. Cold blooded murder. 'The Purging' they called it, and purge they did." He shuddered.

"Well," Mrs. Brody chimed in, "for all the good it did them. They've got witches amongst them again, don't they girls?" She laughed heartily, patting Jane on her back. "I hardly doubt that these soft townsfolk are capable of burning anyone at the stake in this day and age."

The mood lightened slightly, but the stories haunted me. I made a mental note to do some more digging, but I was sure there was nothing to be found on it at the local library.

The conversation turned back to the Shadow

Festival, and we all started chatting again excitedly. We were all looking forward to it, despite the protests from the men sitting around us.

The festival was a chance for us to potentially meet others of our kind, and we were eager to get back upstairs and chat about it. Mrs. Brody, for some reason, didn't seem thrilled, and her mood darkened at the very mention of it. I made another mental note to ask her what the deal was some other time.

CHAPTER FOUR

"WELL, THAT WAS AN INTERESTING EVENING," JANE said, as we hung out in the third-floor lounge after dinner.

I picked absent-mindedly at the peeling purple paint on the window frame, swaying my right leg outside the large open window frame. I was desperate to get to the library and see if I could dig anything up about Brimstone Bay's dark history, but the library was closed until Monday morning, so I had two full grueling days to get through before I could go look.

I had of course done a quick internet search right after dinner on my laptop, but I came up dry.

Jane's stomach growled, and we all turned to her. I laughed.

"What?" she said defensively. "I'm still hungry. I really wanted that damn pie."

"Yeah, what the hell was that about?" I asked.

Mrs. Brody had carefully laid out the spiced pies before her guests but snapped when Jane tried to eat one.

Rory shrugged. "I dunno, but I wouldn't touch anything sweet that comes out of that woman's kitchen."

"Well, technically she didn't bake them herself," I said. "But you've piqued my interest. Why not?"

Rory smirked but held her silence. All three of them looked like they were going to burst with laughter, I noticed, but no one said anything. I looked around the room, waiting for one of them to break. Someone always breaks.

As expected Jane was the first, collapsing in a fit of giggles on the ground. "Oh my god, remember that time at the antique store's fundraising bake sale last year?"

"How could we forget?" Rory laughed. "We spent three weeks doing hard-core damage control after that incident."

"What incident?" I asked insistently. "What the hell are you guys talking about?"

Jane could barely contain herself. "Mr. Hampton held a party to raise money for the shop, and Mrs. Brody offered to bring in muffins."

"Mr. Hampton's fundraisers are always so dull," Bailey continued, "so Mrs. Brody decided she was going to liven things up a bit by spicing up the muffins with worm's wort sprinkles."

They all laughed mercilessly, in too much of a fit to continue.

"Worm's wort?" I asked. "So, she wanted everyone to feel euphoric? Why?"

Jane wiped the tears away from her eyes. "She thought that if everyone was stoned, they'd be more inclined to spend money, I guess?"

"Only," Rory continued, "she accidentally used devil's root instead!" The girls couldn't contain themselves, each one of them rolling on the floor, holding their stomachs because they were laughing so hard.

"She spiked the muffins with a paralyzer?" I asked, absolutely shocked. "People didn't eat them, surely?"

"If only," Rory managed to squeak out. "Luckily she didn't prepare it correctly, obviously thinking it to be worm's wort instead, so she only managed a light sleeping draught."

"Oh, my god," I replied. If they hadn't all been in such hysterics, I wouldn't have believed what they were saying.

"The muffins were the biggest hit of the bake sale, but within ten minutes of the event starting, half the town had collapsed onto the ground, asleep." Bailey sat up, recovering slightly from her laughing fit. "Mr. Hampton thought it was some sort of protest. He was livid, and we had to convince him that it was a local school group practicing a play."

The girls all collapsed in yet another fit of giggles. I just stared incredulously. "And he bought that?" I asked.

Rory nodded. "Well, what else could it have been? Witchcraft?"

I couldn't help but laugh along with them at the sheer ridiculousness of the story.

"It took nearly an hour for everyone to wake up again, and the consensus among them was that they must have had all fainted from the heat." Rory rolled her eyes. "People can be so thick."

I shook my head incredulously. "So... No harm done, then?"

Bailey shrugged. "Well, it took us weeks of spreading rumors that some school kid has spiked the punch and that, mixed with the heat from the sun, was what caused the fainting. Some bought the story of the school group, though."

"Surely some people suspected Mrs. Brody," I said. The other girls nodded.

"Yeah, well, some did, but the majority the people here think witchcraft is a myth, remember, so those that do suspect rarely voice their opinions," Rory grinned.

"Huh," was all I could manage while trying to imagine the scene playing out.

The memory of smelling the devil's root earlier in Mrs. Brody's kitchen came back to me, and I wondered what the woman could have been up to this time. I wanted to bring it up, but I thought better of it. Mrs. Brody still had all her wits about her, despite her age, and I doubted very much that she would have accidentally mistaken worm's wort for devil's root a second time.

THE FOLLOWING WEEK dredged slowly on, the anticipation - or dread, depending who you speak to - of the Shadow Festival growing stronger as the event drew near. I had busied myself with outlining a few articles in advance, so come time for the event I wouldn't be scrambling for ideas. The day had finally arrived, and even though I was prepared, I could feel my nerves going haywire in the pit of my stomach.

The weather was getting cooler, which was fine by me, as I prefer sweaters and mulled wine to tank tops and iced tea any day.

I arrived bright and early at the office to gather some things before heading to the main event area to catch the opening announcements. I desperately needed a coffee, though, and headed downstairs for a Triple Americano once I had packed my bag.

Ryan was standing outside the café with two

other guys. I noticed the door to the café behind him was closed, and there was a 'please come again' sign hanging in the window.

I raised my eyebrow at Ryan as I walked up to him and his friends, holding my arms up as if to ask what's going on.

"Sorry, River, we're closed for the opening event," he said apologetically.

"Aw, what the hell, Ryan?" I demanded, putting my hands on my hips in an attempt to look stern. He knew I needed my coffee every morning. Bad things happened when I didn't get my coffee.

"Don't talk to my bro like that," a tall, scruffy-looking guy said to me, puffing his chest out in attempt to look intimidating, I imagined.

I raised my eyebrow at him, unsure how to even respond to that.

"Dude," Ryan said, jabbing his friend in the ribs with his elbow. "Sorry, River," he muttered.

The same tall, dark-haired guy took one more step towards me, looked down at me and said simply, "Who the hell are you?"

"Who the hell are you?" I snapped right back at him.

"You country girls need to show some respect. In the big city, women know how to treat a man with the respect he deserves." He spat on the ground next to his feet.

"Oh yeah? What city, big guy?" I snarled back at him, refusing to be intimidated by a thug. Poor Ryan looked terrified and just stood there watching the scene play out in front of him.

"Boston."

Oh yeah? Well, I gotcha beat, buster. I looked up at him and smirked, but said nothing. He glared down at me even fiercer, obviously not used to girls standing up to him.

One of the other guys stepped forward putting his hand on his friend's shoulder. "Relax, man." He ran his hand through his dark sandy hair and reached his other out to me.

I accepted the offer and shook his hand.

"My name is Jordan O'Riley, nice to meet you," the sandy-haired guy said. His hair hung loose and messy in front of his icy blue eyes.

I smiled at him. "River. Pleasure."

Ryan stepped forward, finally gaining the nerve to speak. "These are my friends from when I was staying with my mom in Boston. Jordan and Brett. They came out to check out the festival and to catch up. We haven't seen each other in a few years." He eyed Jordan, stepping ever so slightly between myself and his good-looking friend.

I was pretty sure the festival had already gone through Boston just a few weeks prior, but whatever. I nodded at Ryan and said, "I see. Well, I'm heading there now to catch the opening announcements. You guys care to join me?"

"Sure," Ryan said, moving to follow as I turned to walk down the sidewalk. His two friends followed close behind, muttering amongst themselves about something to do with small towns. I ignored them.

"Well this morning is sure going to be a lot harder without that coffee," I said to Ryan, glancing over in his direction. He blushed, and stared down at his feet as he walked.

He shrugged. "Yeah, sorry about that. Dad wanted to check out the festival, and didn't think I'd be able to manage the café all on my own if we got a sudden rush."

"That's fair, I guess." We walked in silence down the main street towards the abandoned house at the end of Pine Court and Jackson Avenue where the event organizers decided to set up their haunted house. It was the main event that everyone was looking forward to.

I breathed in the sweet smell of the early autumn air, relishing the fact that my favorite season had finally arrived. I wouldn't have to deal anymore with the sweaty summer weather and humidity.

I could sense the tingling of magic as we got closer to the haunted house, and a large crowd gathered ahead of us waiting for the announcements that would open the festival for the next week.

I eagerly glanced around, trying to see if I could

pinpoint where the magic was coming from. I could sense at least half a dozen other witches around us. There was a strange, unfamiliar magic that I could sense too, but I couldn't put my finger on what it was. When we finally arrived at the crowd, I turned to Ryan and told him that we could meet up later, but for now, I had to go stand in front so I didn't miss anything for the paper. I ruffled through my bag as I pushed my way through the crowd to the front, and brought out my pad of paper and my recording device.

"River, over here!" Bailey was waving from across the crowd, and I could see the rest of my housemates making their way through the people towards me. I smiled and waved back, recognizing the excited glint in their eyes. I felt it, too. There is magic around us, and we weren't in the house. It was a brand-new experience for us, and I was both excited and nervous at the same time, unsure what this week would bring.

The house was successfully spooky looking, and the decorations scattered around the town were incredible. If they looked this good in the morning light, I couldn't imagine how great it would look at night. You could tell a lot of time and effort went into transforming the town overnight into a ghoulish ghost town, ready for all manner of creatures.

The house in front of us, which normally stood empty since its last owners moved out a few years ago; had been covered in cobwebs, fake blood, and all sorts of other creative decorations. The windows were already boarded up, which contributed to the spooky atmosphere of the place. They made a really good decision by choosing that place for their haunted house. I was used to this sort of scene at Halloween, but it felt weird being surrounded by all those decorations while the sun was still bright and shining. I changed my focus to the events at hand, drawing on my journalistic experience in readying my pen hand to take notes as soon as the announcements began.

"River!" a small voice called from behind me. I turned to look and saw Roger pushing through the crowd towards me. I sighed, having completely forgotten that he was coming.

"My aunt said that you could use an assistant," he grinned up at me once he made his way to the front of the crowd.

"Oh, she did, did she?" I eyed him suspiciously.

He nodded, beaming up at me, his eyes sparkling. I sighed again. "Well, I guess so. But be quiet, and stay close. I don't need any interruptions while I'm working. If I need something, I'll ask you, okay?"

He nodded eagerly, bouncing up and down on the balls of his feet. He looked 19, but acted 12, I thought to myself. Poor kid probably had a hard time at school.

I smiled, though, despite myself. It was nice seeing someone get so excited about this sort of thing. It was a refreshing change.

The crowd hushed as a tall, pale man in a long black cloak and bloodshot eyes walked out of the front door of the house and stepped onto the platform at the foot of the front stairway. "Ladies and gentlemen of Brimstone Bay," the man announced, and then cleared his throat dramatically. You could hear a pin drop, the audience was so quiet.

"I stand here before you today, an undead man having returned from beyond the grave. This festival celebrates all that is paranormal – the mystical witches, the fierce were-creatures, the powerful undead, the lingering spirits, and all those that are still unknown to us." The crowd would clap after the announcement of every paranormal creature. I rolled my eyes, knowing that in any other circumstance people would either scoff at you or run away in sheer terror. But because this was a "show", everyone seems really into it. Let's hope this loosens them all up a little bit, and will make them more open to alternative lifestyles in the future.

"I hereby declare that the 75th annual Shadow Festival is officially open here in Brimstone Bay, Maine. I invite you all to walk through our haunted house, taste our delicious foods from around the globe, interact with all manner of creatures, and truly enjoy your time while frequenting this Fair. But be warned, not all is that which it seems. Be sure to stay together in groups, be aware of your surroundings, and allow yourself the enjoyment of being frightened, as this festival is meant to educate, entertain, and scare in equal measure. Welcome to the Shadow Festival." The man bowed deeply, turned abruptly and disappeared up into the haunted house, the door closing automatically behind him.

The crowd erupted in applause, everyone pushing their way to the front of the line to experience the haunted house firsthand. A short woman came pushing forward, wearing a badge that said Shadow Staff pinned to her black cloak, and she stood next to the door preventing people from coming in.

"Mr. Mayor! May I invite you, your staff, and members of the press to have first access to the haunted house. Members of the public will be allowed to enter shortly after that." When the crowd continued to push forward, she spoke a little more aggressively. "You will all get your turns, do not fret. Please backup and make way for the mayor."

The crowd grudgingly parted to allow him to pass through. He took two steps up the front stairs, turned towards the crowd and smiled at me while I snapped a quick shot of him in front of the haunted house. He winked at me, turned, and then led the procession into the house. I tucked my camera back in my bag, hanging onto the notepad and pen so I could jot down notes as we walked through the haunted house. I then raced up the stairs after him to experience what would be my very first paranormal haunted house experience.

CHAPTER FIVE

THE FRONT DOOR CLOSED BEHIND US AS THE GROUP entered the building.

The house took on an eerie silence once the front door had shut. All sounds of the crowd outside had been muted, and the only noises escaping from the rooms beyond were faint creeks and a bubbling sound.

I had to admit, they did a wicked job with this place. The house itself was an early Victorian from around the late 1860's. It hadn't been maintained, so it was perfectly rickety and decrepit - the event organizers didn't have to do much in that regard. The house was full of numerous rooms of varying sizes, all connected together through large double door openings, typical of the Victorian style.

Drapes, spider webs, and other creepy things had been hung within each doorway, blocking the view from room to room. This added to the suspense of the experience, not knowing what lay in the room beyond the one you were currently in.

Mayor Scott stood at the far side of the entrance foyer and motioned for me to go first. "Might as well get the money shots for the paper before anyone else goes through." His two assistants obligingly stepped aside, relief shown clearly across both of their faces. They obviously weren't thrilled with the idea of going into the haunted house first.

I nodded, placed my notepad and pen back in my bag and retrieved my camera. Noticing that the teen had followed me in, I tossed my bag to Roger so that he at least looked somewhat useful.

I led the way through the large rectangular doorway into what once would have been the large living room. The room now seemed to be a witch's den, complete with a bubbling cauldron, stuffed cat statues - at least I hoped they were statues and not real stuffed cats - and hundreds upon hundreds of dusty old bottles, all scattered around the floor in disarray.

I froze as I stepped into the room. Walking into that much magic was like walking into a brick wall. I eyed the small grey-haired woman who stood hunched over behind the cauldron, and she winked at me. She knew full well what I was. I couldn't help but smile. Glancing up I saw a number of figures floating above us. Faint, the spirits obviously weren't keen on making themselves known. I could make out the details of a few young men and women, circling above us. None of them bothered to make eye contact with me, and I wondered if they were there as part of the show, or just lingering around because of the presence of magic. Either way, none of the rest of the group could see them so I moved on.

I stepped cautiously into the room, and the rest of our group followed close behind. "Whoaaaa," I could hear Roger say from behind me, obviously thrilled with the first room. He wanted witches, and he got witches.

The woman stirred the bubbling contents of the large cauldron as I made my way slowly around the room, inspecting the contents of the few vials that were still sitting on the shelves. I was careful not to step on any of the empty ones on the floor, but from the clanging noises behind me, I could tell that no one else was attempting to be as cautious.

Matching the colors of the bottles' contents to the labels, I assumed that each bottle held the actual ingredients they so claimed. Eye of newt, vampire bat blood, devil's root... all seemingly from spooky tales, and all extremely powerful in potion-making.

My gaze traveled up to one of the cats perched above the window, and looking into its life-like eyes, I doubted very much that it was a stuffed toy. Probably just temporarily petrified with a spell, I suspected. I nearly screamed when the cat winked at me, but luckily my breath caught in my throat.

Everyone jumped back in fright as a form emerged from the shadows of the back corner of the room. A tall, thin woman with waist-length white hair and a long, crooked nose walked forward with a handful of empty vials. She walked up to the cauldron and proceeded to fill the vials while muttering an incantation of some kind under her breath. I couldn't make out what she was saying, but even having been surrounded by witches as a child, the sound sent shivers up my spine.

When all five vials were filled, the witch turned to us and handed us each a vial in silence, then retreated back to the corner of the room and disappeared into the shadows once more.

We all looked at each other, unsure what to do with them. I sniffed my own, trying to place the familiar smells. I highly doubted the event organizers would allow the witches to give an actual magic potion to the guests, but I recognized the scent in the vial and tried my best to put my finger on what it was.

I squeezed my eyes shut and took another deep inhale over the cauldron, then relaxed as I finally realized what it was.

Lavender, rose petals, and orange peel. It was tea. I laughed out loud. "Drink it, it's okay."

Mayor Scott raised his eyebrow at me but then

proceeded to slam back the vial in one go. Roger had drunk his immediately after his was handed to him, not even bothering to question the contents. The mayor's two assistants, Rachel and Tanya, sniffed the contents of their vials suspiciously, reluctant to drink the warm liquid.

I wiggled my fingers at them jokingly. "It's a calming potion. Ouuuuuu." Both girls stared at me, wide-eyed.

I sighed and rolled my eyes. "It's lavender tea," I said simply. Realization dawned on their faces, and they seemed to relax and drink the tea.

I shook my head and then diverted my attention back to the room, taking the scenery in, in all its spooky glory. A witch's house was, of course, nothing like this, movies and television obviously grossly exaggerating the darkness for story telling's sake, but it still felt like home to me somehow.

The cloaked woman behind the cauldron raised her arm slowly, wisps of smoke from the cauldron trailed her hand as it moved, and motioned towards the next room.

As instructed, I led the group through the cobwebbed doorway but halted immediately when I noticed three old women blocking our way.

"Uh…" I said, putting my arm out to stop the rest from bumping into me.

"What are you waiting for, let's go," Roger said, eagerly. I glanced back at him and realized he couldn't see the women. Looking around at the rest of our party, I doubted any of them could see them either.

I looked closer at the women and sensed a transparency about them. Ah, they were ghosts.

They obviously didn't seem to want to move, so I gritted my teeth and walked right through them. I shuddered as I passed through. That was *not* a pleasant experience.

This room was colder, somehow, and felt far less familiar. It was also pitch black, and I could barely see two feet in front of me. I stepped aside to let those behind me come into the room. I felt a surge of power course over my skin, like a jolt of electric energy, but it was like nothing I had ever felt before. I looked around the room curiously, trying to track the source of the magic, but it seemed to just hang in the air all around us, impossible to identify.

Mayor Scott shivered audibly as he walked into the room, and immediately started pacing back and forth. I could sense his discomfort.

As my eyes adjusted, I noticed a long, dark box along the side of the room. A coffin. Apart from that, the room was empty and unadorned, with nothing but the musty, faded wallpaper peeling from the walls.

We all gathered around the coffin, awaiting what came next.

Minutes ticked by, and nothing happened. I

could sense the electric energy in the room growing stronger, and my skin burned from its touch. The sensation got so strong, it was nearly unbearable. I rubbed my arms to try and dissipate the feeling, but it didn't help. Glancing around the room, I could tell that I was the only one that could feel it, though.

Another few minutes went by, and still, nothing happened. Tanya sighed, picking at her nails in boredom.

I nearly suggested moving through to the next room, when the top of the coffin make a loud creaking noise, and we all jumped back in surprise. Slowly, the lid slid sideways and fell with a loud thud between the coffin and the wall.

Everyone took another step back except for me, as I was mesmerized by the sheer power that I could sense coming from within the coffin. The prickling on my skin stopped, and I could feel the power delving deeper into my skin. My blood felt cold, and I was entranced.

A pale-faced man slowly sat up within the coffin, his back rigid as a board. His eyes were open and lifeless, staring forward as his body lifted from the wooden box as if pulled by invisible strings. He stopped, frozen, floating a foot above the coffin in mid-air.

"Cool," I heard Mayor Scott whisper from behind me. He was obviously impressed at the show. I was, too, but more so at the magic than at the spectacle, knowing full well that this was no stage trick.

Rachel and Tanya both gasped loudly as the man's head spun sideways with impossible speed, his black eyes staring at each of us in turn. His body turned to face us as well, but slowly and controlled.

The body glided forward and came to stand before us. The man nodded his head at the mayor, and I absentmindedly lifted my camera to snap a quick photo without taking my eyes off the creature in front of me. I would have to remember to go back to the previous room and take a photo there, as well. Seems I was too distracted to do my job.

The man's power pushed against me, and I resisted the urge to step back. He turned his head toward me slowly and held my gaze with otherworldly stillness. I swallowed, staring up into the endless black pits that were his eyes, trying my best not to shake.

I had never been this close to a vampire before.

Without pulling his gaze from mine, he motioned his arm to the next room, and the group immediately sped off through the doorway, eager to put distance between themselves and the vampire man.

Once the room emptied, the vampire shut his eyes and bowed his head to me. I blinked as if just released from a trance. I backed away and turned to join the group in the next room. I shook my arms out as I walked, trying to rid myself of the prickly magic that lingered on my skin.

The energy in the next room wasn't much different. However, looking around at everyone else in the room, I could tell that I wasn't the only one who sensed it.

Mayor Scott was standing in front of the group, the hairs on his arms standing on end.

I walked up beside him and saw what everyone was staring at. A large black-haired wolf was pacing around the room in front of the group. After a witch and a vampire, I wasn't too sure why a wolf would be such big deal, but hey - everyone's got their weaknesses.

I glanced sidelong at Mayor Scott, who emitted a low growl from deep within his throat. I raised my eyebrow, curious as to why this was affecting him so much.

I crouched down to look closer at the pacing wolf, who snapped his head in my direction and looked at me with his piercing yellow eyes. I stared back eagerly. There was something going on behind those eyes - those weren't simply the eyes of an animal. I smiled to myself, I'd never met an actual werewolf before.

The Wolf made his way to the middle of the room, and everyone stepped backward, backs pressed against the walls of the room. As if on cue, the wolf began to grow, disgusting popping and snapping sounds came from within it as its form changed from beast to man. The hair on its body receded, and its four legs transformed into human limbs as it slowly stood up straight, and turned to look at us. Pain filled his eyes momentarily, before getting quickly back into character and snarling menacingly at the group. Roger reached for my hand and squeezed it, more for his benefit than mine, I'm sure.

The wolfman then grinned a toothy grin and walked past each of us, sniffing, trying to intimidate us. It worked.

He then turned and walked out of the room, and I let out a breath I didn't know I was holding.

The tension in the room eased, but I noticed Mayor Scott was still on edge. I nudged him with my elbow, looking up at him with raised eyebrows. He smiled half-heartedly at me and shrugged. I had no idea how people could come up with a theatrical explanation for that one, which is why I supposed everyone seemed so intimidated by the show.

We all took a moment to collect ourselves, Rachel letting out a nervous giggle once we all seemed to calm down a bit. I smiled at the group, lifted my camera and made them all pose for a picture. "Smile," I said. No one smiled. Great journalism, I thought to myself sarcastically.

I led the way down the hallway towards the next room, careful to avoid the maze of cobwebs and slimy ribbon attached to the walls and ceiling. We approached the end of the hall and were met by a wall of opaque smoke blocking our view into the next room.

I glanced back. "You guys ready?" Everyone nodded, albeit reluctantly. I grinned. People would be talking about this for years, and I was already formulating an article at the back of my mind about the successes of the haunted house.

I stepped forward through the smoke and was knocked sideways by something large and heavy that came swinging down in front of the doorway like a pendulum. It was heavy enough to knock me off my feet and into the side wall, where I banged my shoulder painfully.

"Ow, shoot," I said, rubbing my shoulder as Mayor Scott helped me to my feet. Obviously, the event organizers hadn't timed that one very well.

I stepped back to analyze the hanging object in front of us.

It was a woman, I noted, pale as the moon and hanging by her neck from a rope. She had a piece of red tape covering her mouth and was barefoot.

We all stood and watched, waiting for the show to continue. We waited, and nothing happened. I reached forward to see if it were just a prop we had to walk through, but the solidity of the body told me it was real. I inspected the hanging figure, dressed in a torn dress with bloodied hair concealing her face.

Rachel's nervous giggles picked up again behind me, but a nudge from Tanya silenced her.

Something didn't seem right. I wasn't picking up any tingle of magic emanating from the woman. Instinctively, I extended my magical senses to her, feeling around for some sort of inkling of what she was. I had never learned how to do this specifically; I think it's just a sense that all witches are born with. It allows us to recognize other magical beings without having to get too close. I tried again to feel for something, anything.

Nothing. My senses picked up nothing. This woman was human, but any force of life that once filled her soul had been torn away. There was an emptiness that I could feel from within her. I stared, realization slowly dawning on me.

I screamed, a blood-curdling scream that I didn't know I had in me, tumbling backward desperately into the people behind me.

That wasn't a prop from the haunted house. It was a dead body.

CHAPTER SIX

Mayor Scott's fingers dug painfully into my shoulder as he tried to steady me.

Roger was kneeling down behind me with his face in his hands, and Tanya was on the floor with Rachel who was in hysterics.

"Get them out of here," I said coolly, eyes fixated on the hanging corpse in front of me.

"I've got it," Roger said, who stood up and led the two girls out through the way we came in through.

The lights came on, and the room lost most of its spookiness. The werewolf man came running into the room and stared at the corpse in disbelief.

"She's not ours," he said quickly.

I sensed Mayor Scott bristle at the man's arrival, his body stiffening uncomfortably.

I glanced at him curiously, but he avoided my gaze.

"Lock the door," I said to him. "Make sure no one else comes in."

He nodded and ran out to take care of it.

I stepped closer to the hanging female body in front of me to get a better look. The girl was wearing a torn dress, and her hair was sticky with blood. Her head lolled to the side from the rope around her neck, and she had dark purple circles under her eyes. Her feet were bare, and her toes glittered with shimmery pink polish.

"I'll call the sheriff," Mayor Scott said and walked into another room to make his phone call.

I was alone with the corpse. I closed my eyes and extended my senses out towards the body again. I tried to concentrate and felt my power move through her. At first, I felt nothing, but after a moment's concentration, I began to sense a small inkling of something.

It wasn't magic, but it was the faintest hint of a life force. She was definitely dead, but I didn't think she had been this way for that long

I heard voices growing louder from the next room, and was impressed by the sheriff's timeliness.

I frowned when Ryan and his friends came walking into the room.

"How the hell did you guys get in here?" I demanded, crossing my arms.

"Rumor has it your boyfriend got spooked by a body and ran away with the girls," the tall, dark-haired guy said with a smirk.

I glared at him. "How the hell did you guys get in here? The door is locked."

"The cellar," Ryan's good-looking blond friend, Jordan, told me. "Easy."

I have no idea how they knew to come in through the cellar. I didn't even know there was a cellar. I continued to glare.

"Is... is that a real body?" Ryan asked, his face ashen.

"Cool," the dark-haired guy said.

"No, not cool. This woman is dead," I snapped, moving to put myself between him and the hanging corpse. "Now. Get. Out."

Ryan took a step back and mumbled to his friends that they should leave.

Jordan stepped forward and put a hand on his friend's shoulder. "Let's go, man." He seemed awfully calm given the fact that they all just walked into a room with a hanging corpse.

Mayor Scott walked back into the room, and said flatly, "Out."

The three guys turned and left without a word. God, that man had power.

He called back to them as they left. "Don't go far."

He turned to me with an angry look on this face. "Who were they?" he asked.

I shrugged. "Ryan Bramley and his friends from Boston, apparently." I tried to sound disinterested, not wanting him to think I had anything to do with them coming in here.

"Why are they here?" he asked.

I shrugged again. "Apparently to see the festival."

"No, I mean…" he was cut off when more voices sounded from the front room, and I hoped, this time, it was the sheriff. I recognized the rough, lazy voice as it got louder - definitely the sheriff.

Sheriff Reese and two of his officers came into the room and fell silent as they set eyes upon the corpse.

"Jesus," one of the officers whispered.

It was a pretty shocking sight.

The sheriff shook his head. "This isn't right. Things like this don't happen here in Brimstone Bay."

Not that you would think, anyway, I thought to myself. If anything Mrs. Brody's guests had said was true, this is exactly the kind of thing that would happen here.

"Cut her down," Sheriff Reese instructed.

"Wait," I said quickly, stepping forward towards the corpse. "Shouldn't we at least inspect the scene, first?"

The Sheriff ignored me, and I immediately lifted my camera to snap as many photos as I could. At least this way we have a documented record of the scene to inspect later.

The two officers carefully cut the body down and laid her on the floor. I bent down to get a closer look at her face. Jesus, this wasn't a woman, it was a kid. This girl couldn't have been more than fifteen.

"Who could do something like this?" I whispered as the blood drained from my face. I felt dizzy.

Mayor Scott put his hand on my shoulder. "Let's go outside to get fresh air, and let the boys work."

I nodded, thankful for the excuse to get out of this place.

We walked out the way we had come through the house, and the sun nearly blinded me as we made our way outside.

I noticed Bailey, Jane, and Rory standing back from the crowd, and I went to join them. Mayor Scott busied himself with speaking with the town's folk, encouraging anyone without any information to go home.

Mrs. Pots was standing with the girls, her arms wrapped tight around a pale-faced Roger.

"Is it true?" she asked me immediately. "A murder, here? In Brimstone Bay?"

I nodded and turned my attention to my housemates.

All three of them looked at me expectantly. I sighed, unsure how much I should divulge at this point in time. "A girl has been murdered. We don't know any more than that."

Rory gasped, and put her hand over her mouth. "Is it anyone we know?" she asked weakly.

I shook my head. "No one I recognize."

"The officers will want to speak with you," I said to Roger. His face grew even paler if that was even possible. "Don't worry, we did nothing wrong. Just answer their questions truthfully, and you'll be allowed to go home."

The sheriff and his two officers were coming out of the house, and Mrs. Pots led Roger back toward the crowd.

I noticed flashing lights approach us from behind the house, and saw a hearse park at the end of the back lane.

Jane looked at me, concern spread across her face. "This isn't good, River. This is not going to help the town's perception of the paranormal. Any trust we may have maintained from the very few in this town will have vanished after something like this."

I nodded. "I know. But until we have more information, there's nothing much we can do about it."

Sheriff Reese walked up to me, and the girls turned to leave. "I'll see you guys later," I said to them as they walked away. Rory glanced back at me, a worried look in her eye.

"It's okay, everything will be all right," I lied.

I turned to the sheriff expectantly.

"My boys are going to stay here to interrogate the crowd. I'd like you to join me at the morgue."

I nodded and followed him to his car. I imagine word of my double major in criminology had spread. Otherwise, I wasn't sure why he would trust me with something like this.

As we passed Mayor Scott, he said to the sheriff, "I'll stay behind and help with the interrogations." He turned to me and added, "River, I'd like to have a meeting in my office first thing tomorrow morning before anything gets put in the paper, okay?" I nodded. We would have to be careful about how we handled this, I understood.

I was amazed that most of the crowd had dissipated. For a town so obsessed with gossip, it was a testament to Mayor Scott's abilities that he managed to convince them to go home. I knew for a fact, though, that half the town was on the phone with each other, discussing the day's events.

Sheriff Reese and I rode to the morgue in silence, and I played the scene over and over in my head. A dead body in a haunted house. What is the expression people always say? The press will have a field day? Well, good thing I was the only press in this town.

I was thankful that the sheriff allowed me to join him in this. We had grown to be good friends since I moved to Brimstone Bay – although he still insists on me calling him Sheriff. We would often have coffee together at the café below the paper's office, and I would help him solve his crimes. Well, by crimes I mean the occasionally vandalized street sign or missing antique. Years of journalism school has trained me to be inquisitive, and I've developed very keen problem-solving skills. More often than not, though, I would just help him with his crossword puzzles.

Sheriff Reese pulled the car up to the front door of the morgue, and a man I didn't recognize was waiting for us outside.

"Sir, you're going to want to see this," the man said, and turned to lead us into the building. We followed him through a series of small rooms and hallways, and I thought that this would also make a stellar venue for a haunted house.

We arrived at a small room at the back of the morgue, and the man locked the door behind us. The corpse was lying on the table top and was covered in a thin white sheet that was pulled down just enough to reveal her face.

The girl looked so innocent, and I felt mildly sick to my stomach looking at her.

"We estimate she's around thirteen years old.

Identity unconfirmed." The sheriff nodded and made his way around the table to inspect the body.

I realized I had left my backpack with my notepad and pen with Roger, so I resigned to just taking a ton of photos for later reference. It was not going to be fun reliving this again when it came time to write my story.

"I wanted to wait until you had arrived," the mortician said and proceeded to remove the red tape from the girl's mouth. I gasped at what he revealed.

The girl's mouth had been sewn shut with what appeared to be fishing line. I covered my mouth and willed myself not to be sick.

"Cut it off," the sheriff instructed. The mortician reached for a small pair of scissors, and slowly cut the line from the girl's lips. Once removed, he carefully opened her mouth to inspect inside, which looked to be quite a difficult task.

"Nothing out of the ordinary," he remarked. The sheriff nodded, and I snapped a photo.

"That's not the worst of it, though, sir," the mortician continued.

We both looked up at him expectantly, and he moved to the other side of the corpse and lifted the body, flipping her face down.

He lowered the sheet to reveal the girl's mangled back. I was frozen in place and found myself unable to even grasp what I was looking at.

"What in the bloody hell is that?" Sheriff Reese asked, bending over the girl's body.

"I'm not sure, sir," the other man replied. "Looks like some sort of symbol."

I regained my composure, what little bit I had left, and stepped closer to the body.

The skin on the corpse's back had been carved into some sort of strange, bloody symbol. I swallowed hard, tension building in the pit of my stomach. The symbol was of three circles, each within the other, and a cross cut through. I thought I recognized the symbol from somewhere, but I couldn't place it. I knew I had never come across anything here in town, given the fact that our library is extremely limited and poorly stocked.

I had an idea. I whipped out my phone and snapped a photo of the gruesome symbol with the shitty camera on the back of my phone, and immediately texted it to Riley. *Do u recognize this? Pls look up @ library for me.* I quickly turned my phone off and slid it back into my back pocket. "Just for reference," I said to the sheriff, who didn't look impressed.

"Do you recognize this symbol?" he asked me.

I shook my head. "Never seen it before."

He sighed, and sat down in a chair pushed up against the back of the room. He rubbed his eyes with the palms of his hands and exhaled a deep breath.

"Okay, here's the problem."

I raised my eyebrow. What did he mean, 'problem'? There was a dead girl on a table in front of us. The problem was obvious.

I held my silence and waited for him to continue.

"It's safe to say this wasn't an accident. The fact that she was hung from a rope in a public place suggests that whoever did this was trying to make a statement."

I nodded, agreeing with him.

The mortician continued his analysis. "The markings on her back, whatever the bloody hell they mean, also suggest that the killer was either trying to convey a message, or…"

"Or performing some sort of ritual," I finished.

He rubbed his eyes again, and then looked up at me, a defeated look in his eyes. The sheriff was no idiot, and I knew he suspected the girls and me to be witches. He, of course, had never said anything or asked, which I always appreciated about him, but I know that he had a feeling. And now was not the time to hold anything back.

"What can you tell me about rituals?" he asked me.

I shook my head. "Nothing, Sheriff." I was telling the truth. "I really don't think this has anything to do with the people who came with the Shadow Festival. I don't recognize the symbol. The purpose of the event here is to share the world of the paranormal with the rest of society, and murder at the event would be very bad for business."

"I agree. Then who? Or what?" he asked.

I shrugged again. "I have no idea. But whoever did this, did it with a purpose."

The Sheriff stood up. "A purpose, indeed," he said. "Someone doesn't make a statement this grand and then disappear. I suspect we'll be seeing more from whoever did this."

"Another murder?" I asked, shocked. The mortician's gaze went from me to the sheriff and back again. His eyes grew wide as we spoke.

The Sheriff nodded. "I would suspect, yes. If not that, then something else dramatic. People like this want attention, they want a show. We are going to have to be extremely careful, and we may have to shut down the festival."

I sighed, knowing full well that it would likely come down to this. So much for convincing the town of the goodness of the paranormal.

CHAPTER SEVEN

THE SHERIFF DROPPED ME OFF AT WORK AFTER THE inspection at the morgue was finished. I didn't want to have to think about the story I would have to write, so I went into the café instead, which thankfully had been re-opened.

I really needed that Americano.

Mr. Bramley was standing behind the counter and regarded me gravely as I walked in. "Is it true?" he asked.

I nodded. "Unfortunately, yes."

He sighed and shook his head. "Terrible. Just terrible." He began preparing the espresso for my drink automatically. "Triple?"

"Yep, it's that kind of a day," I said, then sought out a place by the window. The view of the main street was concealed behind overgrown flower planters. Massive colorful flowers and vines grew along the entirety of the window, and I was thankful for the privacy. I heard a loud meowing noise through the window and noticed a small gray cat chewing on the leaves of one of the vines.

"Hey there, little guy," I said through the window, tapping my finger on the window pane. The cat watched my finger, mesmerized, then went back to chewing his leaves.

I settled back into the comfy booth and checked my phone. Seven texts from Riley, all along the lines of *WTH is that* and *More info, plz.*

I texted back: *Just a research project, can you help?*

My phone buzzed back immediately. *Sure, but that better not be an actual body, River.*

I laughed to myself. Not exactly the best text message to receive without an explanation.

Just a pic, I texted back.

Craig Bramley brought over my coffee, and to my delight placed one of his fancy imported cakes in front of me. I never bought them of my own will, as I felt I would be betraying Mrs. Pots and her cakes, but man were they ever good.

Mr. Bramley went back to fussing about behind the counter when Ryan and his friends walked in, and I did my best to look busy on my phone, but they came to join me at the booth and sat down anyway.

I looked up expectantly, not saying anything.

"You don't look so good," Ryan's dark-haired friend said. "Afraid you'll be next?"

Ryan elbowed him hard in the ribs. "Brett, dude, what the hell?"

Brett laughed. "Just teasin' her. God, you small-town folk are so uptight."

"I think that's what they say about us city guys, too," Jordan chimed in.

"Four coffees, dad," Ryan called to his dad across the café. He turned to me. "Care if we join you?"

"Actually, I was just leaving." I stood to leave, but Jordan reached out and grabbed my arm. "You should stay," he said, winking at me. "Tell us what you found out about the woman's murder."

I pulled my arm away from his grip, not impressed in the slightest.

"That's all there is to know," I said sharply.

I turned to leave, and Jordan added, "Anything unique about the body?"

I eyed him suspiciously, wondering how he would know to even ask that.

"Nothing that we could see." He looked let down. Good.

I left the café without another look back at them and called out a "thanks" to Ryan's dad as I left.

I walked home quickly with my head down, not wanting to interact with anyone else. I was mentally and physically exhausted, and all I wanted was to sit down and drink my coffee in peace. I knew that once I got home, the girls would pester me about the murder, but that sure beats dealing with Ryan and his pushy friends.

I heard the same little meow noise behind me as I walked away from the café, and I turned to see the little gray cat was following me. I bent down to scratch its ears, and it rolled onto its back for a belly rub.

"Well, aren't you just a friendly little guy," I cooed to it, scratching its fuzzy white tummy. I noticed he didn't have a collar and figured he must be a stray. "You look pretty damn good for a stray," I said to him. He purred under my touch.

"I've gotta go home, now," I said to it. "Go back to where you came from."

I walked away, but the cat followed me. I hoped it would lose interest eventually, but the damn thing followed me all the way home. When I finally arrived at the house, I gave it one last scratch. "Sorry, buddy, you've got to stay outside." I closed the door behind me, and the cat sat outside on the steps, looking up at me through the window with big, sad eyes. Damn, the last thing I needed at that moment was a guilty conscience. I shut the blinds and tried to put it out of my mind. I had bigger things to deal with than a clingy cat.

The house was surprisingly quiet, and I relished in the peace as I desperately threw off my clothes and jumped in the shower to try and wash the memories of the day from my skin. The memories, unfortunately, didn't go away, but the steaming hot water felt really good.

I then heard a loud bang from far below me, and I knew where the girls were. I laughed and stepped out of the shower so I could dry off and go join the fun. Every now and then we all would have a 'witch off' with Mrs. Brody. What's a 'witch off'? Well, I'm glad you asked.

Essentially, we all would do our best to out 'witch' each other - with harmless spells, of course - by showing off our potion and spell casting skills. It always ended up in complete mayhem, and it was a total blast. I needed the distraction right about now.

I was not prepared for what I walked into, though.

Tiny little Mrs. Brody was backed up into the far corner of the room looking distraught, her hair a flamboyant neon pink color. Jane had lost her eyebrows, Bailey had grown antlers, and poor Rory had sprouted a bright green mustache. Not only that but the little gray cat that followed me home was sitting on the kitchen table, with a bow tie tied around its neck, watching the fun with interest.

"Er... what's going on here?" I asked, doing my best to contain my laughter.

"Get. It. Off. Of. Me." Mrs. Brody said through clenched teeth.

Rory crossed her arms stubbornly. "Not until you get rid of my mustache!"

"Now," Mrs. Brody snapped. "Get. It. Off. Right. Now."

Jane and Bailey were doubled over in a laughing fit of hysterics, obviously not helping the situation.

"I think it suits you," I offered to Mrs. Brody. The pink actually looked good on her.

"Not. The. Hair." She breathed again through clenched teeth. "Get. It. Off."

"Not until you get rid of my mustache, old woman," Rory said menacingly.

Both witches were at a standoff, staring daggers at each other.

"What is she talking about?" I asked Jane, who had regained her composure somewhat.

"Oh, that's not a *tail* I should tell," Jane said, her face straight.

Rory calmed down enough to add, "Let's just say she was at the *tail* end of a bad spell."

Silence filled the room for a moment, and then the two girls burst into another monstrous fit of hysterical laughing.

I stared at Rory in disbelief, finally catching on. "You didn't?" I asked, biting my lower lip to not join in the laughter.

"She started it," Rory stated.

"Let me see it!" I turned to Mrs. Brody, who was looking angrier than I'd ever seen her before.

She slowly turned around and revealed what looked like a long monkey's tail sticking out from her dress.

I couldn't contain myself any longer, and joined the two girls on the floor, holding my stomach desperately, laughing harder than I had in a long time. I wiped the tears from my eyes as I tried to catch my breath. Realizing that neither Mrs. Brody nor Rory were going to let up first, I stood up, tried to collect myself, and put on a mock stern face.

"Honestly," I said, crossing my arms. "You are both acting like children."

Growing up in a house full of experimental and particularly creative witches, there were a few key spells you mastered early on. One of which was particularly suited to situations like this.

I closed my eyes and concentrated, and then muttered the incantation from memory. It had been nearly 15 years since I'd had to use that spell, but it was still fresh in my memory. I focused on Mrs. Brody's pink hair and nasty tail, Rory's mustache, Jane's missing eyebrows, and Bailey's antlers.

I opened my eyes and the room filled with a flash of light, and when my eyes adjusted everything was back to normal.

"Hey," Mrs. Brody barked at me. "Give that back."

She snapped her fingers, and her hair returned to neon pink.

"Oh, sorry," I laughed. "It is a good look for you."

"I know," she snapped, then busied herself in front of the kitchen sink, peeling some kind of funky-looking vegetable.

I sat down at the kitchen table and scratched the cat behind its ears. The cat didn't seem too perturbed at the nonsense that was going on around him. "What are you doing here, little guy?" He rolled over again onto his back for more tummy scratches.

I rolled my eyes. "What a little suck up you are."

The girls came and joined me around the table, each taking turns giving the cat belly rubs.

"You doing ok?" Bailey asked me, looking concerned.

I nodded. "Yeah, I'm fine. A little rattled, but fine."

"Any updates on the murder?" Rory asked.

"Well," I started. I wasn't sure how much to tell, but given the circumstances, I figured I might as well be honest. "This is classified information. Keep it between us, okay?"

They all nodded eagerly.

"The body had some sort of symbol cut into its back," I said, then paused. "I don't know what the symbol meant, but it suggests the killer was trying to make a statement, and it's rare that these sorts of cases are one-offs..." I trailed off, the dread I felt earlier returning to the pit of my stomach in full force.

"What do you mean?" Rory asked, concern drawn across her face. "You mean there will be more of these?"

Mrs. Brody joined us at the table and sat down, looking utterly dismayed. "I doubt it was coincidence, occurring right when the festival came to town."

"Do you think it was one of the festival people?" Bailey asked. "Why would they do something like this?"

"Of course not," snapped Mrs. Brody. "More likely someone wanting to make it appear as if it were them. Put the blame on the paranormals. It's not a new thing, dear." She sighed, memories of a darker past obviously haunting her. I remembered the stories her spirit friends told us the other night and felt a chill crawl up my spine.

"It's possible," I said. "We don't want to come to any conclusions before we've had a chance to investigate further."

"Are we in danger?" Jane asked, her face had drained of all its color.

"I think it's safe to assume, at this point, that everyone is in danger. Just be careful, stick together and don't go anywhere that could get you in trouble, okay?" I looked at each of them in turn, waiting for their agreement.

"I have a meeting with the mayor and the sheriff first thing in the morning. We'll figure this out," I added.

"What are you going to say in the paper?" Bailey asked.

I shook my head. "I have no idea. But we have to be careful about it. I think that's why Sheriff Reese is letting me stay so close to this case. The way we communicate these events to the town will have a huge effect on how things will be, going forward."

I lay my head on my arms, and the little cat walked up to me on the tabletop and rubbed its body against my face.

"Who let him in?" I asked, giving yet more tummy rubs to the little fuzzy thing.

Everyone looked at each other, but not one of them had an answer.

Bailey shrugged. "Must have jumped in a window."

I glanced around, noticing each window was closed. "Uh-huh," I said, not believing them.

"He obviously likes you," Rory said, beaming. "You should keep him. We could use a cat around the house to scare off the spirits." She laughed.

"Hey now, none of that," Mrs. Brody interjected. She wagged her finger at the cat. "No scaring away my friends."

The cat meowed in reply. "I didn't know cats

could see spirits," I said, eyeing Mrs. Brody. "Since when?"

"Since always, dear," she said, petting the cat on the head. "You've obviously read the story books. Where do you think those books get their ideas from?"

Huh. Who knew.

"Well, little guy," I said to the cat. "Welcome to the family, I guess." He meowed, and rolled over on his back for more belly rubs.

"Speaking of ghosts," Rory said. "If she was murdered, couldn't we just ask her ghost what happened?"

I didn't even think of that. "Do all murder victims turn into ghosts?" I asked, curious. The haunted house was full of ghosts, but none that I could tell matched the profile of the murder victim.

As if on cue, one of the ghosts from the dinner party emerged from the living room.

"Excuse me, don't you knock?" Mrs. Brody chided the man, as he approached the table. He ignored her.

"To answer your question, yes, all murder victims become ghosts," he said matter-of-factly. He must have been eavesdropping from the next room. How convenient.

"Hi, Mr. Richards," Rory said, smiling at the man.

"Hello, my dear," he replied, tipping his bowler hat in greeting.

"You can't just come around uninvited, you know," Mrs. Brody said sternly to the man.

"I am a ghost, madam," he replied. "I can go anywhere I please, and I wish you luck in stopping me."

"Hmph," Mrs. Brody replied, turning up her nose. "We'll see about that."

I laughed, curious as to how she could possibly control the whereabouts of a ghost. I wouldn't put it past her to try, though.

"If I wanted to track down a specific spirit," I asked Mr. Richards. "Where would I look?"

"Oh, a number of places, I suspect," he began. "Near the body, at the murder site, at a location dear to the person while they were living…"

I sighed. "So, anywhere."

"I would start at the murder site, as that's where the spirit will first appear."

"We're not sure where that was," I said, defeated. "I don't think the murder happened where the body was found. There was no blood. Not that I noticed, at least."

"I could have the boys do a sweep of the town if you like?" he suggested.

I sat up straight. "You can do that?" I really didn't know much about ghosts, I realized.

"But of course," he said to me. "What do you

think we do with our time? Float around in one place all day?"

I never thought of it. I guess I assumed ghosts just sort or disappeared when not interacting with anyone who would see them. I kept that thought to myself, though.

"I'm coming," Jane said immediately.

"Me, too," Bailey added.

"Ditto," said Rory.

I sighed. "I guess that means I'm coming, too. But we need to be discreet about it, okay? We'll just go for a stroll through the town, and Mr. Richards will report back to us."

"Works for me," Bailey said, excitedly.

"That work for you, Mr. Richards?" I asked him. He saluted me and vanished through the wall.

CHAPTER EIGHT

THE SUN WAS STARTING TO SET AS WE MADE OUR way into the town's center. The street was nearly deserted, which was nice as it would mean fewer questions directed at us as to why we were wandering about aimlessly.

We had no real direction in mind, I figured we would just walk down the main street, and Mr. Richards would check in with us with any new information.

We arrived at the main street and stopped to wait on the sidewalk a few blocks away from my work. I hoped Mr. Richards would at least let us know what his plans were, so we weren't just walking around in aimless circles.

"Ladies," a low voice said from beside me. I jumped, clearly not expecting anyone to be so close. I turned to look where the voice had come from and noticed an extremely faint shimmer of Mr. Richards' floating body. He was so transparent in the low, glowing sunlight that I could barely make him out. To be fair, I hadn't known ghosts could even go outdoors, let alone be seen in daylight. My serious lack of knowledge about ghosts would have to be rectified if I planned to continue living in a house full of witches.

"Hi, Mr. Richards," I said politely, looking around to make sure no one else was close. "What's the game plan?"

"I've got some of the fellows on board," he said, clearing his throat. "We will search through the town and see if we can spot any trace of the girl."

"Oh River, dear," a voice called out from behind us. Damn, bad timing.

Bailey casually raised her finger to her lips, signaling to Mr. Richards to be discreet.

Mrs. Pots came running out from her shop to join us on the street. "I delivered your bag to your work, River. JoAnn put it on your desk for you."

I watched her, wide-eyed, as she came to stand directly next to Mr. Richards. He eyed her up and down curiously, then proceeded to pretend to look at his wrist, that was missing a watch mind you, suggesting he was eager to stay on schedule.

Mrs. Pots didn't notice, and my suspicions that she had been lying about being able to see spirits were confirmed. I smirked, wondering why on earth she would insist on such a thing.

"Thank you, Mrs. Pots," I said kindly. I didn't say anything else, hoping she would take the hint and leave. We had business to attend to.

"Poor Roger is in hysterics," she added conversationally. "I haven't been able to get the poor boy to calm down since the incident. He would love it ever so much if you came to see him."

"Sure thing, Mrs. Pots," I said. "I'll stop by tomorrow after my meeting with the mayor. You can tell him we'll grab a coffee or something."

"He'd like that," she said, and then added, "What is happening to our quiet little town? Murder, here, in Brimstone Bay." She made a sweeping motion with her arms, and I noticed her left arm go right through Mr. Richard's body.

She turned to leave, then paused. Looking back at us, she asked, "Did you feel that? What a strange chill."

Shit, well maybe she could sense spirits after all.

I shook my head. "Just the breeze. Bye Mrs. Pots, I'll see you tomorrow." I waved, encouraging her to go.

She shook her arms out dramatically, as if to ward off the breeze, and went back to her shop.

I let out a breath to ease the tension that I had been holding. I looked at Mr. Richards, who was still eagerly inspecting his watch-less watch hand.

"Don't forget the haunted house," Bailey said to him as if our conversation hadn't been interrupted. "Given that's where the body was found, it probably makes sense to start there."

"Indeed," the ghost said. "I shall check there myself."

"There were a bunch of ghosts there this morning. I had noticed them before we found the body," I added.

The transparent spirit nodded. "I will check back shortly. Don't go far." He left before we could say anything else.

"Be gentle if you find her," I shouted after him, then glanced about to make sure there was nobody around to have heard me.

We continued walking down the street, looking for traces of spirits as we went. The warm glow of the setting sun made it difficult to see much of anything, and we gave up trying after a few minutes of squinting.

We walked along the street slowly, being sure to stay visible in case any of the spirits had anything to report back. As we neared the site of the haunted house, though, I noticed a small group of people lurking around the front of the building.

I brought my hand up to my eyes to block out the sunlight, and could barely make out who it was.

"Shoot," I said, dropping my hand back down to

my side in exasperation. It was Ryan and his friends. What were they doing there, I wondered?

"Who is it?" Rory asked, squinting herself to try and see.

"It's Ryan Bramley and his friends from Boston."

"What are they doing at the haunted house?" Bailey asked.

I shrugged. "I was wondering the same thing."

"Should we go see?" Rory asked again, still squinting into the setting sun.

"No, definitely not," I said flatly. "I've had enough of those guys for one day. Let's just wait here."

We found a bench the next block over and sat down to wait for news.

"What are we going to do if we find her?" Jane finally asked. The other girls turned to me expectantly, obviously wondering the same thing.

"I have absolutely no idea," I said honestly. "I'll have to find out who she is, of course, and hopefully get some clues as to what happened."

I sighed, feeling beyond overwhelmed by the events of the day. God, this day really needed to end.

Rory put her arm around me and gave me a comforting squeeze. "You've got this," she said. "You were born for this stuff. It's why you came, isn't it?"

I laughed. "Well not exactly for this." I

wondered what it would have been like if I had gotten a job in a big city. I would be writing about murders all the time, I imagined.

"I guess I never expected to be involved in anything like this, especially on my own. There's no one else at the paper who has any real formal training, especially in this sort of thing, so I'm going to have to blunder through this myself and hope I don't screw it up too badly."

"I just feel sorry for the girl's parents, whoever they are," Jane said, staring off into the sunset. "I can't imagine what they are going through right now."

"They probably don't even know she's dead," Rory said. I didn't know whether that was comforting or horrifying. Either way, we were going to have to figure this out so they could get peace.

About half an hour had passed before Mr. Richards returned. He was joined by a few other transparent forms, but I couldn't make out who they were.

"We found the girl," he said, puffing out his chest with pride.

I stood up. "Really? Where?"

"She's hiding in the attic of the house," he said. "She shied away from me, as I expected she would. She wouldn't say anything, either."

"What did you say to her?" I asked, encouraging him to go on.

"I told her not to be frightened, and to remain where she was." He added, "I'm afraid there's not much we can do for her. Poor thing is frightened beyond repair."

He turned to leave and began floating away.

"Wait," I said hurriedly. "Please, tell the girl I want to speak with her. Tell her I will meet her tomorrow morning just before first light." Hopefully, no one else will be out and about that early in the morning.

"Tell her I want to help her, and that everything will be okay," I added

He nodded and disappeared.

"He's always in such a hurry," Jane mused.

"Ghosts," Rory sighed.

"We should get home," I said. "I don't think it's a good idea to be out after dark. Not until we find the killer."

We walked home quickly, eager to get back to the safety of the house. I glanced back towards the haunted house as we left, and saw the four guys were still there. I paused and watched them suspiciously for a moment, then turned and jogged to catch up with the girls.

I figured it was safe to say that that had been one of the longest days of my life, and I was thankful it was finally almost over. I said goodnight to the girls and locked myself in my room. I really just wanted to be alone for a while.

Only, I wasn't alone. The little gray cat was sitting on my bed waiting for me.

"Now how did you get in here?" I went to join him on my bed. He purred as I scratched him behind the ears, and he rolled over on his back wanting a belly rub. "You are a funny little guy, aren't you?" I rubbed his belly obligingly, and his purring grew even louder.

"Do you have a name?" I asked. He didn't respond. Obviously, he was a cat.

"What about Whiskers?" he rolled back onto his feet and looked at me, tilting his head sideways. "No? Then, how about Mittens?" He continued to watch me.

"Well, you look like you rolled in a fireplace. What about Soot?" At that, he meowed. "Alright, Soot it is." I scratched his ears, and he purred.

After the day I had, I was happy for the silent companionship. No interrogations, no pestering questions, just company and cuddles.

"You know what?" I said to the cat, as I laid back on my bed feeling defeated. I kicked off my shoes and pulled a pillow down under my head. "You're the best thing to happen to me all day." I set my alarm for four o'clock in the morning, closed my eyes, and instantly fell into a deep sleep.

CHAPTER NINE

FOUR O'CLOCK CAME WAY TOO SOON. I FELT LIKE I had barely closed my eyes before my phone buzzed next to me, jarring me awake. It took me a few moments before I remembered why I had set my alarm so early, but once I remembered the dead girl, my mind was instantly alert.

I had fallen asleep in my clothes, so I quickly changed, brushed my teeth, and quietly tiptoed out of the house. My hair was a disheveled mess, but I had grown used it by now. The air was chilly, and the streets were nearly pitch black.

There was a calm silence in the town as I made my way to the haunted house. The sky was still dark, and the sun wouldn't rise for yet another hour or two. The street lamps offered enough light to see, though.

The town was deserted, and the house had an

eerie stillness to it, cordoned off by police tape. Knowing that there were ghosts in the house added to the eeriness, but given my purpose in going there, I didn't let that detract from my mission.

I didn't want to be caught trespassing, so I leaned against the fence on the side of the house, where I noticed one of the windows wasn't boarded up. I stood there and waited, hoping the girl's ghost would come to me.

Relief flooded through me as I saw the form of a young girl emerge in the window. She stared out at me looking frightened.

"It's okay, there's no reason to be afraid."

The girl didn't move and continued to stare at me.

"My name is River," I said calmly. "I'm here to help you. Can we be friends?"

She nodded to me. Good, we were off to a good start, at least.

"Can you tell me your name?" I asked.

She shook her head.

I sighed. "Something bad happened to you, and I'm going to help figure it out. Okay?"

The girl nodded.

"First, I need you to tell me your name so I know what to call you."

She shook her head again. Damn, this wasn't going to be easy. I didn't really have any experience dealing with living children, let alone dead ones.

"Is it because you don't want to, or because you don't know what your name is?"

A few minutes went by, and I watched the girl struggle to try and say something. Finally, she whispered, "I don't know."

Crap. Okay, back to square one.

"Do you know how you got here?"

She shook her head. I let out a breath of air - this was going to take a while.

"Let's play a game," I said, trying desperately to come up with a plan. The girl smiled and nodded.

"Okay, you get to ask me any question you want, and then I ask you a question. It can be any silly question you want. Does that sound fun?"

The girl shrugged. "Why don't you go first," I offered, then waited patiently for the girl to ask something.

"What day is it?" she asked. Okay, not the most creative question, but I guessed I should cut the kid some slack.

"It's Tuesday today, the second day of October," I said. "All day long."

She smiled. "My turn," I said warmly. "What's your favorite color?"

"Blue," she said shyly. Great, at least she still remembered things about herself. That was a good start. "I love the color blue," I said to her as she smiled. "Your turn."

"Why am I here?" Ouch, my heart broke just a little bit.

I tried to be as gentle as I could. "Well, that's what I'm trying to figure out, sweetheart. I just need you to answer a few more questions and then I will hopefully be able to give you that answer, okay?"

She nodded.

"Do you go to school?" She nodded again. "What's the name of your school?"

"Beacon Park," she said, then frowned. "I don't want to go back to school."

"Well, what if I told you that you never had to go back to school again?" I told her, smiling. It was sad but true. She beamed up at me. "Really?"

"Promise," I said. "What grade did you just finish?"

"Grade 9."

"So you just finished your first year at high school?" She nodded. Ugh, the first year of high school was never easy, and this poor girl would never get to experience all the fun that you could have as you climbed the high school food chain. At least I knew where to start looking for more information.

"Do you live with your parents?" I asked, hoping to gain some insight into her family.

She nodded. "I live with my mom and dad and my grandma."

The sky was beginning to lighten, and the early

morning commuters were beginning to come out. I brought my phone out and pretended to talk into it, so people wouldn't ask any questions if they saw me talking to myself outside of the haunted house.

"Do you remember your name now?"

She paused. "Jessica."

I smiled at her. "Great job, Jessica. Do you have a last name? Or do you just have the one name like Beyonce?"

She giggled at that, and then said, "Of course I do. Sturgess."

"Jessica Sturgess," I said out loud. "What a pretty name. Now I can try and get some more information on why you're here, okay?"

She nodded shyly.

"Do you remember anything about what happened?"

She shook her head. "I remember going to sleep excited because my mom had just taken me Halloween decoration shopping like she always did at the end of September. I went to bed late after helping her put up some of the decorations, and the next thing I know I'm here in this house, surrounded by weird floating people who keep talking about weird things."

Awesome, that gave us at least a window of time when the murder would have happened. Sometime between the end of September and yesterday, so that gave us a very short window.

"Jessica, I'm going to have to go and do some research, okay? Can you stay here and wait for me to come back later?"

She nodded. "Promise me you won't leave the house, okay? I need to know where to find you later."

"I promise," she said. "Don't take too long."

I smiled. "I won't. And when I come back, I'll hopefully have more information about why you're here."

I waved goodbye, sad that I would be leaving her alone in the house with the other spirits, if they were even still there. What a strange environment to find yourself in as a young girl.

I headed towards my office to pick up my backpack that Mrs. Pots had dropped off for me and to grab a much-needed coffee. I couldn't remember the last time I was awake so early, and I knew my energy would crash soon.

I was not pleased when I noticed Ryan's friend Jordan leaning against the front door to my office.

"Couldn't help but notice you hanging around the haunted house this morning," he said conversationally, a sly smirk spread across his face.

"And how exactly did you *notice* that?" I asked, putting emphasis on the word notice. "What are you doing out so early, anyway?"

"Just out for some early morning exercise," he

said and flashed a winning smile at me. I did my best not to notice how attractive he was.

I glanced down at his jeans and sneakers. "Not really dressed for exercise there, Jordan."

He shrugged. "Okay, you got me. Just wanted to come say hi."

"Well, hi," I said, trying to push past him so I could get to the door.

"Hi," he said to me, but didn't move out of my way.

"I need to get into my office," I said sharply.

"Have coffee with me," he replied.

"What? No, I have to work."

"Let me buy you one little coffee."

I sighed. "You can buy me coffee, but I won't be able to stay and drink it. I have a meeting with the mayor about the murder."

That seemed to peak his interest, and he stood up a little straighter. "Oh, yeah? Got more information about the killer?"

"Why are you so interested?" I asked.

He shrugged. "Just curious. I hope they find who did it soon."

"Uh-huh," I said, eyeing him cautiously. "Are you going to buy me that coffee, or what?" I asked, hoping that it would at least make him get out of my way.

"Oh. Right. Yeah, of course." He moved to step towards to neighboring door of the café.

"I'll be down in five minutes," I said, then took advantage of his not standing in my way and opened the door and ran up the stairs to my office before he could say anything.

I locked the door behind me at the top of the stairs and ran to my desk to turn on my laptop. I only had a few minutes to find out everything I could about Jessica Sturgess before my meeting with Mayor Scott and Sheriff Reese.

Luckily, her name was all over the Internet. *Missing Girl Disappeared from Home* was the first hit on Google, and the link brought me to a digital poster with Jessica's face plastered on the front. Bingo. I printed the page out and stuffed it in my backpack, then proceeded to skim through some of the other articles. She had been missing for a few days, and by the looks of it, there have been no leads. Her poor parents must be having an awful time.

I checked the clock on my phone, and I only had 15 minutes before I had to be at the mayor's office for our meeting. I shut my laptop and zipped it into my bag, then went downstairs for that dreaded coffee with Jordan.

He was sitting in one of the booths with two large to-go cups in front of him, with a pleased smile on his face. "I got you a pumpkin spice latte. Girls love those," he said to me.

"Oh, thanks," I said, glancing over at Mr.

Bramley behind the counter. He shrugged at me and went back to fussing about behind the counter.

No, not all girls liked pumpkin spice lattes.

I pretended to take a sip. "Yum, delicious," I lied.

He smiled, obviously pleased with himself.

"Ryan really likes you, you know," he said conversationally. Ugh, really? That's what he wanted to talk about?

"Okay. So why are you buying me coffee then?"

He shrugged. "We're not that close."

"Look, thanks so much for the coffee, but I really do have to go to this meeting."

"Sure, no problem. Good luck with everything." He sounded like he genuinely meant it. I smiled back.

"I'll see you later. Going to go say hi quick to Mr. Bramley." I got up and leaned against the counter. Mr. Bramley discreetly swapped my latte for an Americano and winked at me. Pumpkin spice and milk had no business being in coffee, if you asked me. I glanced back to make sure Jordan didn't see, and I waved goodbye to both of them as I turned to leave. Ryan walked in right as I was walking through the door, and blushed furiously as we nearly bumped into each other. He smiled, then noticed Jordan sitting alone at the booth and frowned, putting two and two together. I didn't have time for this, so I pushed past and muttered a quick "See ya."

I sipped my Americano as I walked, deliriously happy for the caffeine fix.

Despite the haunted house being closed, the town was still decorated for the festival. Cobwebs hung from the street signs and lamp posts, and open coffins lined the sidewalk next to the benches. Lots of the shops had joined in the festivities, too, decorating the storefronts with Halloween decorations. It was October, so I guessed this wasn't completely out of character. My favorite part was that at night, fog came spilling out of the flower boxes along the main street, giving the streets a really cool, graveyard vibe.

The mayor's office was just around the corner, and Sheriff Reese and Mayor Scott were already sitting around the conference table at the back of the office waiting for me.

"Thanks for coming, River," Mayor Scott said warmly to me as I sat down across from him. He yawned. It's been a long two days for all of us, and this day was only just beginning.

"I've filled the mayor in on what we saw at the morgue," Sheriff Reese told me. "He's up to speed on the body. Now we just need to figure out who she is and the name of the sick freak who did this to her."

"Jessica Sturgess," I said to the two men. They looked up at me surprised. I opened my backpack and placed the printed out poster on the table. "She popped up when I was searching for missing children online."

The sheriff reached for the paper, inspecting it closely. "Been gone since Sunday," he said from behind the paper. "Went to Beacon Park High School, Haverhill. Anyone know where that is?"

"Just north of Boston," Mayor Scott said. "My sister and her family live near there."

"Boston?" I asked. "Why would the body of a kid from Boston turn up in Brimstone Bay?"

Mayor Scott shook his head. "I have no idea. What I'm more concerned about it making sure that this isn't a recurring event."

"We'll see to that," the Sheriff said confidently. "In the meantime, I'll need to contact the local police in Haverhill and let them know we have something of theirs." He sighed and took the printed poster as he left the office.

I stood to leave as well. Mayor Scott put his hand on mine and said, "River, just one moment."

I sat back down, looking at him expectantly.

"Because of the grave circumstances and severe implications this will have on the town, JoAnn and I have agreed to call in for additional help with the paper."

Um, what? He had better not been saying what I thought he was saying. I stared dumbly at him.

He continued, "I have full faith in your abilities as a journalist, but I think having the extra help will be a really good thing for you. You can lighten your load a bit, and you'll have help from an experienced journalist for the next few weeks."

"I don't really know what to say to that," I said flatly. I was fully capable of handling the situation myself.

"We wanted you to have a comfortable working relationship with the new journalist, so we called NYU and requested one of their more experienced students. Do you know Zack Brendon?"

I gaped at him in disbelief. "You're effing kidding me?"

"I'll take that as a yes?" he asked.

Zack Brendon was a TA in one of my investigative journalism courses. He was a total self-obsessed jackass who was way too full of himself for his own good.

"Yes, I know Zack," I said through gritted teeth. "But this really isn't necessary. I am perfectly capable of handling this myself."

"I know you are," he replied. "He's not here to replace you, he's here to help you. Think of it as a gift from me to you."

I didn't even know how to respond, so I just sat there staring at him. I shook my head. "Wait, you mean he's here already?"

"Arrived first thing this morning."

I stood up, pushing the chair back angrily. I

know I looked childish, but I just couldn't get over what was happening.

I turned to leave, and Mayor Scott added, "I'd like to review the story before it gets published."

I nodded curtly and walked straight out of his office. Zack freaking Brendon, the absolute last person I wanted to see just then. My week just kept getting better and better.

CHAPTER TEN

I DREADED GOING TO THE OFFICE. IT WAS THE LAST thing on the planet I wanted to do right now - I walked so slowly, I might as well have been walking backward. No amount of coffee would have been able to get me through the next few hours.

I mentally prepared myself as I walked, doing my best to see the bigger picture. This was my first big journalist job, and the events of the day before were more serious than anything else that had ever happened in my town before, at least in recent memory. I understood where Mayor Scott and JoAnn were coming from, but that didn't mean I needed to like it.

As I approached the office, I resigned to at least try to work amicably with Zack, then hope that before long he would be on his way back to New York. From what I remembered, he still had another semester left of his Master's degree, so he wouldn't be able to stay too long, anyways. That's what I told myself, at least.

I could see a crowd of people through the second-floor window of our office, and figured JoAnn must have called a full staff meeting. There were two other part-time journalists working at the paper, but we rarely saw each other. Most of us preferred to work from home.

I swallowed my pride as I walked up the stairs. I put on a fake smile as I entered the office.

"River, glad you're here," JoAnn called. "You know Zack, right?"

I extended a hand to him as he walked towards me, but he ignored it and pulled me in for a big hug. I stood, rigid - a hug was the last thing I was expecting, and to be honest, I really didn't feel comfortable with his arms around me.

"So good to see you, River," he beamed at me as he released me from the hug. "I'm looking forward to working with you on these articles."

"Nice to see you, Zack. How long are you in town?" I cut right to the chase. I didn't want any unexpected surprises where he's concerned.

"Not sure yet, probably a few weeks."

I sighed. "Nice, well, I hope you enjoy it here. It's certainly not New York." I hoped he would get bored and leave before those few weeks were up.

"Nah I love it here. I grew up in a town not far from here, actually." Damn, so much for that.

JoAnn called everyone around her desk, and we all pulled up our chairs. The office was tiny, and we didn't have a boardroom or even a communal table. We also only had two desks, and would have to share desks if we all worked in the office at once. That was part of the reason why we preferred working from home.

"Now, I'm sure you're all aware by now about the murder that occurred yesterday morning." Looking around the room, I could see everyone had been kept up to speed.

"Zack and River will be covering the events surrounding the murder, and everyone else will resume their regular weekly assignments. I expect you all to offer Zack help when he needs it, as he is unfamiliar with the town and we are the only people he knows so far." She smiled at him, looking absolutely radiant. Oh great, just what I need. My boss had a crush on her douchebag journalist.

Zack turned to me and said, "I'm going to go spend some time in the library. You good to meet up later and go over some notes? I have a few ideas for the direction of the articles." Of course, he did.

I nodded. "Sure. Meet here this afternoon?"

We all left the office, and I was thankful that the meeting only lasted a few minutes. With any luck, the few weeks with Zack would be quick and painless, although part of me seriously doubted that.

I picked up another coffee on my way home, desperately needing to keep up my caffeine intake if I was going to make it through the rest of the day. My head was whirling with the events of the past 24 hours, and I really needed to pull myself together.

As expected, Soot was waiting for me at the foot of my bed when I got home. I collapsed on my bed, and he came up and curled next to my face. I scratched his ears and turned my face into his soft fur. "You always know how to make me feel better, don't you?" He meowed.

I rested a few moments, then noticed a savory smell coming up through the floorboards. I took a deep sniff and sighed. "Ah, lunch!"

I picked up the cat and went downstairs to see what Mrs. Brody was cooking up. I wasn't surprised to see Bailey, Jane, and Rory sitting around the kitchen table. They always seemed to congregate wherever there was food.

"Smells good, Mrs. Brody," I said as I walked into the kitchen. She often left the door to her basement apartment open so we could come and go as we please. "What's cooking?"

"Oh, hello dear," she said warmly to me. "Just a pot pie, nothing special."

"Sounds good to me," I said. I hadn't realized

how starving I was. Your body could only go on so long, living off of nothing but coffee.

"How was the meeting?" Rory asked, and the room quieted as everyone else turned to look at me for news.

"We've identified the body." I reached for a piece of bread in the basket on the table. I took a big bite and nearly swallowed it whole. "Some poor girl from around Boston."

"Boston!" Mrs. Brody exclaimed. "How in the devil's name did she get all the way up here?"

I shrugged. "That's what we're trying to figure out."

"It's so sad," Jane said. "So young."

I nodded, taking another bite of bread.

There was a knock on the side door, and we all turned to see who the unexpected newcomer was. Everyone we knew was already there, pretty much. "Hello?" Mrs. Brody called out.

"It's Roger," a small voice said through the door.

"Oh, dammit," I muttered. I totally forgot I was supposed to go see him today.

I sighed. "Come in, Roger," I called to the door.

The door opened slowly, and a timid Roger came walking through. He joined us at the table. "My aunt said you were going to stop by, but I saw you walking home. I thought I would come see you here."

I tried my best to smile. "No problem Roger,

have a seat." He looked around the room, beaming at the girls. Not one of us confirmed his suspicions of us being witches, but you could tell by his expression that he had already made up his mind. The poor kid had an obsession.

"Lunch is almost ready," Mrs. Brody said, her voice echoing in the oven. "Hope you're all really hungry."

My phone began buzzing furiously in my pocket, and I saw four text messages come in from Riley.

I swiped the screen on and quickly read through his texts. He had spent the morning at the library on campus and was sending me his findings. I clicked on a link he sent and nearly dropped my phone when I saw where it led.

"Holy crap," I gasped, eyes fixated on the screen. I scrolled down the page, ignoring the questions that came flooding in from everyone else around the table. After I had skimmed through the entire article, I turned the screen off and pushed my phone away from me on the table as if it were a bomb ready to go off.

"The symbol," I said shallowly.

"What symbol?" Rory asked, reaching for my phone.

"There was a shape carved into the girl's back," I said. "It was some kind of symbol, but we had no idea what it meant."

"And?" Bailey encouraged.

"And," I continued. "I now know what it means."

Rory tossed my phone back to me. "Unlock your screen. I want to see the symbol."

I obliged and held up the phone with a screenshot of the symbol. It showed three circles and a cross.

"What does it mean?" Jane looked concerned.

Mrs. Brody had grown silent and stood frozen in the kitchen, her face pale. I suspected she knew what the symbol meant.

"According to the article," I began, "it dates back to an order of witches in Salem. It was used to mark someone who was to be cursed."

I placed the phone on the table so everyone could see the symbol on the screen. "The three circles symbolize the heart, the mind, and the soul. The X marks them as the next victim."

"Witches did this?" Roger asked, looking shocked.

I shrugged. "I don't know. If it was, it certainly wasn't anyone around here." I glanced around the table at my housemates, each looking more concerned than the last.

"That was done by no witch," Mrs. Brody whispered.

"How do you know for sure?" I asked.

"A symbol like that is meant to mark a victim, but nothing more. Once the deed is done, it is finished. There would be no reason to advertise their work after death. It makes no sense."

I agreed. "You're right. Not that I'm agreeing that there is anyone out there that would mark someone with a witch's mark," I eyed Roger. "But if such a thing did exist, I imagine whoever did it would want the evidence hidden, not broadcast to the world."

"If it wasn't witches," Roger said shyly, "then whoever did it sure wanted to make it look like it was."

I nodded to him. "Yes, you're right." The truth was even scarier than the alternative.

"If that is true, then what kind of person would want to pin this on witches?" Rory asked, her eyes full of fear.

"I don't know," I said. "But if that's what happened, then no witch is safe."

CHAPTER ELEVEN

I SAT SULKING AND FEELING SORRY FOR MYSELF FOR a solid hour before Zack returned to the Brimstone Press office later that afternoon. Not only did I have to sit there stewing in my own dark thoughts for an hour, but the walk to work had been an absolute nightmare.

The details of the murder and the symbol found on the body had obviously spread like wildfire through the town. People were literally running away from me as I walked down the street. One woman actually screamed, picked up her small child and ran into a nearby store. So much for the town not believing in witches.

I was eager for this afternoon to be over so I could go back and visit Jessica at the haunted house. If the town was going to start suspecting witches were behind the murder, then it was absolutely crucial for me to get to the bottom of this before any of us are deemed to be suspects. The Shadow Festival was allowed to continue, despite the haunted house being permanently closed, but since the incident, I haven't sensed any other witches in town. They must have vanished after word got out about the murder. I don't blame them.

My only comforting thought was that I was sure most people still really didn't want to believe that paranormal beings were real. I hoped that the religious small town mentality held true, and if things took a turn for the worse, that people would realize how silly they were being, afraid of some superstition that stemmed from stories intended to scare children. I hoped, at least. The biggest problem here was Mayor Scott. If Sheriff Reese decided witches were actually behind this, and convinced Mayor Scott of the same, then I doubted it would be long before the mayor brought us in for questioning. And then boom, right then and there, our whole cover of secrecy would be blown.

I was so lost in my thoughts when Zack came in, that I hardly noticed the extra body in the room. He cleared his throat, and I jumped out of my trance with a jolt.

"Oh, sorry," I muttered, mildly embarrassed. "Didn't notice you there."

"Wow, you must be really shaken up by the murder," he said, taking a seat at JoAnn's desk.

"Am not," I said defensively, aware that I sounded like a stubborn child. "Was just thinking about the article we're going to be writing."

He sighed. "About that... I found absolutely nothing at the library that would be of use to us."

"I could have told you that," I said. "Luckily, I've got some information we can use."

Realizing that I hadn't even told Sheriff Reese or Mayor Scott that I learned what the symbol was, I quickly reached for my phone and texted the sheriff. *Have info on symbol. Meet at my office?*

He replied *OK*, and that was that.

"Sheriff Reese is on his way in. I'll fill you both in at the same time," I said, desperately trying to think of a way to present this information to them so as to not immediately implicate the witch community, or myself, more particularly. "Let's grab a coffee while we wait."

"I'll get them," Zack offered, and left me alone again with my thoughts. I snapped open my laptop and immediately started typing frantically into the search bar, hoping to find any more information on the symbol. Riley mentioned it was simply called the *mark*, which made it difficult to pinpoint in any Google search. But after inputting a few detailed keywords describing the shape, the page became flooded with articles about the occult and the paranormal. I added the words *modern times* to the search, in hopes that I could find something about whether the symbol is still used throughout the modern witch society. The search came up dry, which I took as a good sign.

Zack returned a few minutes later accompanied by Sheriff Reese and Mayor Scott. The tiny office was crowded, but they all sat around my desk, eager for me to fill them in.

"Well?" Sheriff Reese said expectantly. "What have you got?"

I opened one of the better Google images I could find and sent it to print. The mayor reached for the paper as it spat out from the printer, and placed it on the desk in front of us.

"That's exactly it!" The sheriff looked impressed. "What does it mean?"

"It dates back a few centuries," I said, choosing my words cautiously. "It was used as a sort of marker. The symbol meant that you were marked to be cursed."

Zack laughed. "You've got to be kidding me!" I stared at him, eyes narrowing. How he could find this funny was beyond me.

"You don't actually believe in curses, do you?" He rolled his eyes at the idea. I could feel Mayor Scott's eyes on me, but I avoided making eye contact and just stared incredulously at Zack. I forgot this detail about him. Despite having lived in New York City, he didn't believe in witches. At least, not that he would admit.

"Obviously, someone is trying to take advantage of people's stupidity," he said, matter-of-factly. "Just trying to spook people."

"Stupidity is right," I spat at him. Although, his blatant denial about the existence of witches could actually help our case. The last thing we needed was people believing us to be responsible.

Sheriff Reese shook his head. "No, that doesn't make sense. No one recognized the symbol, so using it as a scare tactic seems pointless. I imagine there's some sort of dark magic behind this, whether you choose to believe that or not." Well, shit.

"I don't know," I began. "In my research, I couldn't find any recent precedent for it. The symbol seemed to have disappeared with the dark witch communities centuries ago."

Zack's mouth hung open. "Oh come on, River. Don't tell me you believe in all of this nonsense, too."

Poor, stupid little man.

"Nonsense or not," I said to him, "we know exactly what the symbol means. Or meant, at least, at one point in history. We just need to figure out what the heck it's doing on a body of a thirteen-year-old girl in the 21st century."

"Whether it was intended as a scare tactic or actually meant to mark her as cursed, the fact that the body was left to be found in such a location suggests the killer wanted the message to be known." Mayor Scott had a point.

"What do we put in the paper?" I wanted to make sure we were all on the same page.

"Leave out the symbol," the sheriff said. "Just lay out the basics, who she was, where she was found, and mention that the case is ongoing, and we will have more information soon."

"I think it's too late to keep the symbol secret," I muttered. "Rumor seems to have spread already."

Mayor Scott sighed. "Brimstone Bay is good for that."

"Just do your best to keep the article as clean and to the point as possible. Don't add fuel to the fire," the sheriff said. "I've got a telephone meeting with the local police from her hometown this evening. Hopefully, we can get to the bottom of this before things get out of hand. The last thing we need is for the town to think we have murderous witches on the loose."

"Murderous people pretending to be witches," Zack corrected. For once, I was thankful for his stupidity.

"Either way," I said. "We need to find the killer before anyone else is hurt."

"Or killed," the mayor added.

We stared at each other, fear in both of our eyes. "Or killed," I agreed.

I jumped as the door creaked open, and JoAnn walked into the office.

"Oh lovely," she said, sarcastically. "Thanks for the invitation."

Sheriff Reese checked his watch and stood up. "Sorry Jo, last minute meeting. I've gotta run, the girl's parents are due to arrive tonight, and I need to make arrangements. River will fill you in." He shook Mayor Scott's and Zack's hands, patted JoAnn on the shoulder, and walked out of the office.

I let out a loud, exasperated sigh. JoAnn looked at me expectantly, but I stood up as well. "I'm sorry JoAnn, I really do have to go. Do you mind if Zack fills you in?"

At least this way Zack would explain it to her in such a way that kept the witch community out of it. She nodded, and I grabbed my bag to leave.

"I'll be back tomorrow morning," I said. "Zack, we can compare notes tomorrow and get the article finished in the morning."

He nodded, and I waved goodbye, thankful for the opportunity to get out of the office.

"Come meet me in my office tomorrow so we can talk further," Mayor Scott said as I walked out of the room. I nodded my agreement and left.

I took the long way home as an excuse to stop by the haunted house.

I leaned against the same fence next to the one

open window and pretended to be on my phone as I called Jessica's name.

She immediately turned up at the window, and I smiled. She smiled back at me.

"Hello again," I said warmly.

"Hi."

"How have you been doing?" I asked, regretting it immediately. The girl was dead in a strange house; how did I think she was doing?

She shrugged at me.

"Your parents are going to be coming to town tonight," I told her. She looked like she was going to cry.

"They know I'm dead?" she asked, sniffing.

I nodded. "Yes, they do."

"Can I see them?" she asked, hopefully.

I sighed. "Well, sweetheart, you're a ghost. They won't be able to see you."

"But you see me," she said.

I nodded. "Yes, but that's because I'm different. Most people can't see or talk to ghosts."

"Oh."

"I'm so sorry, Jessica," I said, my heart breaking all over again. "The only thing we can do for them now is to help solve the case about your murder. Answers are the only thing at this point that will give them peace."

"Ok."

"I need your help. I need you to try and

remember everything you can from before you died. Can you do that for me?"

She nodded. "I can try. I don't remember anything, though."

I sighed. "You said you remember putting up decorations with your mom. Do you remember seeing anybody else that night?"

I waited while she scrunched her face, trying to remember. She shrugged, and looked as if she was going to cry again.

"Okay, don't worry about it. I know it's hard," I said. Then I got an idea. "I'm going to go home and see if I can figure out how to jog your memory. I'll be back."

"Can I come?" she asked. I paused. I guess I never really thought of that.

"Uh, sure," I said. "I don't see why not. My friends at home are different, too. They'll be able to see and speak with you."

She beamed at me. "Really?"

I nodded, happy that I could at least offer her that much. "Yep, they're really nice. You'll like them."

She stepped through the wall of the haunted house, and I finally got to get a better look at the ghost. I noticed that the girl's mouth looked normal - no scars or stitches like her body had. Strange, I wonder what that meant?

"What are you looking at?" she asked me, retreating slightly from my blatant staring.

"Nothing, sorry. Do you mind turning around for me?"

Jessica twirled around, and through her torn dress I saw the scars that marked the symbol on her back.

I swallowed hard, trying not to let my emotions show on my face. The symbol must have been carved into her back while she was still alive.

"What is it?" she asked, after twirling around a few times.

"Nothing at all," I lied to her. "Let's go."

We walked in silence through the side streets, the sun slowly setting below the houses behind us.

"Oh look, is that a full moon?" she asked, looking up to the sky.

I looked up to the moon. "It sure is."

CHAPTER TWELVE

THE SKY WAS BLACK BY THE TIME WE MADE IT BACK to the house. I knocked on Mrs. Brody's door, figuring she might have an idea of how to better approach triggering Jessica's memory.

"Come in, come in," I heard Mrs. Brody's muffled voice call from within her apartment.

I glanced at Jessica, then opened the door and led the way inside.

"Well, well, well," Mrs. Brody said as she joined us in the kitchen. "Who do we have here?"

By the look on her face, I assumed she already knew.

"Mrs. Brody, this is Jessica Sturgess," I said, stepping aside so she could get a better look at the ghost.

Jessica stared at her feet shyly.

"Hello Jessica," she said warmly, stepping closer

to the ghost. "My name is Agnes. It's wonderful to meet you."

I blinked and then laughed out loud to myself. In the entire time I've lived here, I never even knew her first name. I smirked.

Mrs. Brody waggled her finger at me. "It's still Mrs. Brody to you, missy."

I nodded. "Whatever you say, Mrs. Brody." I looked down at Jessica and winked, which made her laugh. That made me smile. The more comfortable she was around us, the more likely she would be to remember.

I sat down at the kitchen table and looked seriously at Mrs. Brody. "She can't remember anything about what happened to her, and if we don't find out who did this to her soon, then we're all going to be in big trouble."

Mrs. Brody looked at me. "Yes, dear, I imagine we will be."

"Is there anything we can do to help kick start her memories?"

She walked to the kitchen window and peered out at the sky. "Lucky for us, it's a full moon tonight. I know just the thing, but we'd better hurry. Go get the girls. I'll prepare." She then walked out and left us alone in the kitchen.

"You okay to stay here a few minutes while I go upstairs?" I asked.

Jessica nodded.

I ran upstairs as fast as my feet could carry me, and rounded up my three housemates. They followed me downstairs without question and looked confused when they all gathered around the kitchen table and saw Jessica's ghost standing nearby.

"Girls, meet Jessica," I said.

Jessica smiled timidly.

Rory smiled. "Hello Jessica, my name is Rory. This is Jane and Bailey." She motioned to the other girls in turn.

Jane smiled, but Bailey stared wide-eyed at the girl, then turned to me. "Is that the girl who was murdered?"

I nodded. "We're going to help her remember things, so we can solve the case and be done with it."

Mrs. Brody came back into the room with a large, heavy-looking basket. "Grab your coats, it looks a bit chilly outside."

I eyed her suspiciously, unsure as to what she had planned. But I knew better than to ask, so I grabbed my sweater from my bag obligingly and followed her outside.

She took us down through the long back yard, to the steep wooden stairway that led down the rocky bluffs to the beach below. We all followed in silence, then took our shoes off when we arrived at the bottom of the stairs. The sand was wet and cold between my toes.

Mrs. Brody led us to the fire pit just beyond the bluffs, and with a snap of her fingers, a large bonfire appeared from the ashes.

"Whoa, how did she do that?" Jessica asked, stepping back away from the fire. I guessed I was going to have to explain a few things before we began so she didn't get spooked. I didn't imagine they had very many witches where she came from.

"You know how I said we were different back when we were talking at the haunted house?" I asked.

She chewed her lip but nodded.

"Well, the reason we can see and talk to you is because we have magic." I smiled and then motioned to the fire. "Like what Agnes just did there with the fire."

Her eyes grew wide as she looked back and forth between me and the fire.

"Some small towns don't really know much about it," I added. "But lots of people have magic. We just don't flaunt it in public."

Rory noticed the scared look on her face and added, "It's okay. It's good magic. No need to be scared. We can do stuff like make things fly and sparkle."

She looked over to Bailey, who squinted her eyes at the fire. It began to change color. Pink, blue, and purple flames sparkled and twirled around in the fire pit, looking like a shimmery rainbow.

"Whoa," Jessica said again, this time looking genuinely impressed.

"Come girls, around the fire now," Mrs. Brody sat down cross-legged on the other side of the fire and motioned for us to sit in a circle. "Jessica, too."

"What are you doing, exactly?" I asked.

"Recalling our memories," she replied, her eyes closed tight in concentration.

"What do you mean our memories?" Bailey asked. "We just need Jessica's."

"It doesn't work that way, dear," Mrs. Brody replied. "It's all or nothing. Hope none of you have anything to hide."

We eyed each other nervously. I didn't have anything to hide, but I really didn't like the idea of my memories being put on display for all to see.

"But," Bailey protested.

Mrs. Brody shushed her. "We may witness premonitions as well. Stay focused."

We all sat around the fire in silence, watching her at work. With her eyes closed, she reached into her basket and brought out different herbs one at a time, sniffing each one to make sure she had the right one. She then proceeded to crush them between her palms and sprinkled them over the fire. She muttered an incantation under her breath, too low for me to make out what she was saying.

After about ten minutes, she had completed her

ritual and opened her eyes. "Ok now, I need you grab hold of each other's hands and form a complete circle."

I glanced at Jessica, who I knew wouldn't be able to physically hold our hands, and placed my hand palm open beside her. She lay her hand over the top of mine and did the same to Mrs. Brody on her other side.

"Now close your eyes, and concentrate on a memory. Any memory will do, whatever is strongest."

We closed our eyes, and I focused on the memory of cooking potions with my dad as a kid. There was this one time we made a laughing draught and inhaled way too much of the fumes and we laughed solidly for three days. By the time the magic wore off, I swore I had six-pack abs from laughing so hard.

I felt a warm breeze circling me, blowing my hair into my face. I could feel the magic building around us.

"Open your eyes," Mrs. Brody said.

We did and were amazed at what we saw.

Different images flickered in the firelight, each only lasting a few moments.

"Okay now," Mrs. Brody said quickly. "Each memory will only last a few seconds, so if you recognize it as yours, call it out for us all to hear.

With luck, we'll be able to see Jessica's memories and hopefully gain some insight as to what happened to the poor dear."

Jessica started into the fire, transfixed on the images.

"That's Soot," I said, as an image of my little gray cat appeared in the flames.

"My sisters," Jane said.

"That's my old dog, Baxter," Rory said as the image of an old bulldog flashed before us.

"Ryan Bramley," Bailey said, blushing furiously in the firelight.

"My dad," I added.

"Craig Bramley," Mrs. Brody said.

We all eyed her, and she snapped "oh never you mind," as the image of grey-haired Mr. Bramley passed through the fire. I tried not to giggle.

"Jordan?" I said questioningly, seeing his face before me. That was weird.

"My grandpa," Rory said.

"Holy crap," Bailey said, as an image of two elderly people, a man and a woman, appeared in the flames. Their lips were sewn shut, and they stared out at us with sad eyes.

"Oh gosh," I muttered. "Please say I just imagined that." I desperately hoped that didn't mean what I think it meant. Two more dead bodies, coming our way.

"Kids I used to babysit," Jane said as the image changed.

Jessica screamed suddenly as an image of a person in a black hoodie appeared in the fire.

I turned to her and asked, "Is that it? Is that the person who killed you?"

She nodded slowly, eyes transfixed on the shape in front of her.

I tried to take in everything about the image as I could before it changed. Black shoes, ripped baggy jeans, a black hoodie with the hood up, unfortunately concealing the person's face…

"Mrs. Pots," Bailey said as the image changed.

"My friend Riley," I added, as Riley appeared.

Jessica was shaking. I didn't even realize ghosts could shake.

"That's just about enough, I think," Mrs. Brody announced, and with a wave of her hand the fire disappeared, leaving a few burning embers behind in the pit.

I immediately jumped up and ran back up the stairs as fast as I could manage. We could deal with the identity of Jessica's murderer later. For now, we have two new bodies to look for.

Once I got back into the house, I grabbed my phone and immediately called Mayor Scott. I could at least tell him about the premonition without him thinking me crazy.

The phone rang and then went dead. Shit.

I tried calling again, and the same thing happened. It was only just after midnight, and I figured he would still be awake. I called again, and after the fourth ring he picked up the phone and growled at me. "Not. Now." He then hung up the phone.

"What the hell?" I asked myself out loud.

I sighed, then dialed Sheriff Reese's number. It went straight to voicemail. Great, his phone was off. Just absolutely perfect. I waited for the beep and then said sharply, "Call me. Now." It was times like that that I really missed my old flip phone. It was so satisfying slamming it shut on someone.

I paced back and forth, trying to figure out what the hell I was supposed to do.

I picked up my phone again and texted the Mayor. *I think there has been another murder. Call me.*

I waited, hoping for a reply, but none came.

I felt defeated and collapsed down onto a kitchen chair.

Mrs. Brody and the girls arrived a few minutes later and joined me at the table.

"You okay?" Bailey asked, reaching over to squeeze my hand.

I nodded. "Yeah, I just really wish we could get to the bottom of this before anyone else gets hurt."

"We don't know for sure that those people were murdered yet," Jane offered.

I looked up at her. "You're right. If that's the case, then we need to do everything we can to prevent it." I moved to stand up, but Mrs. Brody put her hand on my shoulder and pushed me back down into my chair.

"We can't do anything about it this instant," she said calmly to me. "You don't know who those people are, and you don't know the identity of the killer. Going out there now is too dangerous."

"She's right," Rory said. "We need to think this through."

I sighed. They were right, of course. I would have to wait until morning, but at first light, I would be on my way to the mayor's office to see what the hell was going on.

"Did any of you recognize the person with the hood?" I asked, knowing full well what the answer would be.

They all shook their heads.

"We don't know for sure that's the killer," Rory offered.

"By Jessica's response, I think it's a fair bet that it was," I said. "And if not, we can fairly confidently say that whoever it was at least has something to do with this. Whether that person was a suspect or a victim, they wouldn't have shown up in the flames otherwise."

I glanced around the room and suddenly realized that Jessica was missing.

"Damn, where did Jessica go?"

No one else had noticed her leave, and we all got up to look for her.

"She's gone," Mrs. Brody said. "Poor thing. Probably scared witless."

Jane rolled her eyes. "How do you spook a ghost?"

"More importantly," I added. "How do you find one?"

"We did it once, we can do it again," Bailey comforted me. "Don't worry, we'll find her."

"I don't blame her for being scared. Those two people spooked me, too," Rory said, lifting her knees up so she would wrap her arms around her legs in the chair.

"Yeah, what was that on their mouths?" Jane asked.

"They were sewed shut," I said. "Jessica's body had the same thing done to it."

Jane blinked. "That's odd. Her ghost didn't have it."

I nodded.

"What does it mean?" Rory asked.

"It means it was done after she died," Mrs. Brody offered, her voice grave.

"Why would someone want to do that?" Rory asked.

Mrs. Brody heaved a heavy sigh. "I imagine they

did it so the ghosts couldn't speak." It took a moment for the severity of her words to sink in.

"So whoever did it didn't want us to be able to speak to them?" I asked, barely believing what I was hearing.

"Thankfully whoever did it doesn't understand ghosts very well," she added. "Or else they would have known that they would have had to do it before they died for it to remain in place in the spirit world."

A shiver crept up my spine. "Okay, so let me get this straight. We have a murderer who knows about witches and ghosts, but not enough to truly understand them. So that removes anyone from the paranormal community off the suspect list. Also, whoever did this obviously wanted to make it look like a witch's ritual with the symbols, and wanted very badly to prevent us from being able to speak to the ghosts to get the truth."

"Alternatively, it could actually be a witch, purposefully making those mistakes to throw us off," Rory offered. She had a point; we didn't want to jump to any conclusions.

I really, really hoped that wasn't the case, though.

We all sat around the table in silence, letting the information soak in. There was a murderer who was trying to frame witches, killing innocent people and dumping them in our town. Well, that's just great.

I leaned back in my chair and rubbed my eyes. It had been an extremely long day.

"I need to get some sleep," I said and stood up to leave without saying another word. I would need at least a few hours if I was going to have enough emotional capacity to handle the next few days.

CHAPTER THIRTEEN

AGAIN, MORNING CAME TOO SOON. I FELT LIKE THAT was becoming a recurring theme, one that I really didn't enjoy.

My bedroom faced east, which meant the morning sun at least helped wake me up. I stretched and yawned, allowing myself a few extra minutes in bed to cuddle with Soot. He had become the best thing about my mornings.

My phone beeped from across the room, and I grudgingly willed myself to get up and start my day.

I made my way across my bedroom and look at my phone. It was a text from one of Mayor Scott's assistants saying he was sick today, and unable to meet.

The hell with that. Sorry, Mayor, you don't have the luxury of sick days when a murder investigation is going on in your town.

Ready to give him a piece of my mind, I quickly showered and got dressed and left the house before anyone else woke up.

It was barely eight o'clock, and the town was still mostly asleep. I took the long way to the mayor's office to avoid having to see anyone on the main street.

The door to the mayor's office was closed, but I could see a light on inside. I knocked, and Tanya, one of his assistants, answered the door.

"I'm sorry, but Mayor Scott is unable to make his appointments today," she said sweetly to me.

I grabbed the door before she had the chance to close it.

"It's important," I insisted. "I need to see him. Now."

She tried her best to close the door, but I was stronger.

Finally, she let me come into the office and closed the door behind me.

"Where is he?" I demanded.

"Mayor Scott is sick as a dog, and can't meet with anyone right now," she said. "Poor guy seems to get sick every month, he really should see a doctor about it."

"Well I'm not leaving," I said stubbornly.

Tanya crossed her arms and spoke through gritted teeth. "Fine then, have it your way. He's all yours." She then grabbed her purse and stormed out of the office. She obviously wasn't having a very good day, either.

I took my jacket off and made myself at home. The mayor must have been in the back room, as the front office was deserted.

"Mayor Scott," I called to the back.

"Not now, River," he called back. "Whatever it is can wait until tomorrow."

"This can't wait," I said sternly. I marched to the back room to see where he was hiding. It wasn't like him to be this standoffish.

I opened the back door, and my breath caught in my throat as my gaze was met by two glowing yellow eyes.

I stepped back. "Mayor?"

Mayor Scott stepped into the light, revealing fangs and an excessive amount of hair growing down from his neck.

"No," I said, raising my hand to cover my mouth. "How?"

The mayor sighed, and sat down in one of the chairs at the back of the storage room.

"I was bitten as a kid," he said. "Full moons aren't exactly a cup of tea for me."

I nodded. "I see that." I examined him up and down. He only demonstrated traces of being a werewolf - he still had the human form of a man. "Why haven't you said anything?"

He shook his head. "I'd rather keep it to myself. I'm sure you can understand."

I nodded again. "Of course."

"Why did you come to see me, River?" he asked with an edge to his voice that I had never heard before.

I blinked, trying to remember why I had come. Oh yeah, bodies.

"Two more people will be murdered. Or, maybe have already been murdered."

He stared at me. "How do you know?"

"Same way you know to avoid a full moon."

He nodded. "I see. Does the sheriff know?"

"No, I couldn't get a hold of him. I don't even know what I would say to him."

"Just tell him you found more research on the symbol or something, anything that will convince him to put out a search," the mayor instructed me. "Call him now."

I reached for my phone and dialed the sheriff's number again. This time, it rang.

"Not a good time, River," the sheriff said to me over the phone. What was it about everyone today?

"Sheriff, it's important."

"Two more bodies were found," he said.

Oh. Well, shit.

I looked up at Mayor Scott, who had heard the sheriff speak through the phone. The superhuman hearing was a bonus of being bitten by a werewolf, I guessed. He shook his head in disbelief and rubbed his eyes as if he hadn't slept in days.

"Where?"

"They were found in two of the coffins on the main street," he said to me. "You had better get down here. We're right in front of the Brimstone Press office."

My phone clicked as he hung up.

"You go," Mayor Scott said to me. "I need another few hours before I'll be fit to be seen by the public."

"Okay, take all the time you need," I said, and turned to leave.

"Call me with any new information," he called to me as I left his office.

A crowd had gathered, and the entire block had been cordoned off with police tape. I ducked under the tape and jogged up to Sheriff Reese, who was standing next to one of the coffins with a few of his officers.

"They were found here this morning," he said to me as I got close. "A man and a woman, look to be in their late sixties."

I looked down into the coffin at a pale-faced man with his lips sewn together.

"Same M.O.," I commented.

The sheriff nodded. "We haven't had a chance to

turn them over yet, but I bet we'll find the same symbol on their backs."

"I think that's a fair assumption," I said.

I felt a knot forming at the pit of my stomach. I really hoped this wasn't something I could have prevented if I hadn't gone to sleep last night.

"Do we know who they are?" I asked.

"Actually, we do."

I looked at him in surprise. "Really? Are they from town?" I didn't recognize them.

He shook his head. "No, but we got a call from the Wells police late last night. Word has gotten out about the last murder, and people are on edge. These two were reported missing yesterday evening. They own a small farm just outside of the town."

"Where's Wells?" I asked.

"South of here. On the drive up from Boston."

"Boston?" I asked. "They're getting closer."

The Sheriff nodded. "We'll have to get the bodies transferred to the morgue so we can inspect them further. You coming?"

I nodded. "Yeah, I'll come."

The day felt like deja vu, driving to the morgue with the sheriff in silence. We needed to find the person behind these killings, because I really didn't want to have to relive this day a third time.

The hearses arrived at the morgue just moments after we did, and I watched as the coffins were carried inside. I took a deep breath and followed them. I readied myself as I knew exactly what waited for us inside.

The bodies were laid on two tables. I walked up to the man to get a closer look at his mouth. The stitches were clean, obviously made after he had died. I don't know why I didn't notice that before.

The officers helped the mortician flip the bodies over so we could get a good look at their backs. As expected, both bodies were carved with the same symbols.

Only, these ones looked different.

"There's something different about these," I commented, looking back and forth between the man and the woman.

"The shapes are the same," one officer commented.

I nodded. "They are. But they're different. Look, there's no blood on these."

"The carvings were made post mortem," the mortician said, inspecting the cut lines. "On both of them."

"Why would these two be different?" I asked, looking up at the Sheriff for answers.

He shook his head. "I have no idea. The poor girl suffered through it while still alive. I don't know what made these two different."

"Could they have died of shock before it happened?" I asked.

"It's possible," Sheriff Reese answered. "Or the killer just got sloppy."

A sloppy killer often leads to a found killer, so that was one point working for us, I supposed.

I stared down at the two corpses, feeling incredibly sad for what happened to them. Why would someone want to kill a child and two farmers?

I hoped we could find their ghosts at least, and with any luck, they would remember something useful. Maybe if we brought all three victims together, their memories would be triggered.

I got out my phone and texted Bailey: *Another ghost hunt. Can you ask Mrs. Brody to find Mr. Richards again? Be home in an hour.*

"We at least know one thing," I said to Sheriff Reese.

He sat down on one of the stools next to the examining table and massaged his temples. The stresses of the past few days seemed to be taking a toll on him. "What's that?"

"We know the symbols weren't actually used as a means to mark these people," I said. "It doesn't make sense to mark someone as cursed after they're dead."

The sheriff nodded. "I guess so. I just want to find this nut job who thinks he's cursing people."

"No…" I started, but then gave up. He obviously didn't understand what I was saying. "What I'm saying is that I don't think this has anything to do with cursing. The person who placed the marks on these people obviously doesn't know how they work."

"And how do you know so much about this?" he eyed me blankly.

I shrugged. "It's amazing what you can find on Google these days."

"Alright well, curses or no curses, we need to find out who did these before another body turns up. The murders themselves are happening closer to town, and we still have no idea why the bodies are turning up here. We don't know if it has anything to do with the damned Shadow Festival, or if that's just a coincidence, and we don't know whether the killings are part of some sort of old dark marking ritual or just some young punk trying to scare people."

I sighed, the tinges of exhaustion finally taking over. "We do know it's not part of some ritual," I insisted, motioning to the symbols on the woman's back. "Can't mark someone for cursed once they're dead."

The sheriff sighed. "Right, sure. Cursing sounds bogus to me, anyway."

I stared at him, not really knowing how to respond. I had thought that he was smarter than that, but I guessed not.

"Either way, we need to solve this before anyone else dies," I said.

He nodded. "That much we agree on."

"I'm going to go do more research, see what other information I can dig up," I said. I didn't feel the need to tell him my research involved searching for ghosts rather than Google.

CHAPTER FOURTEEN

SHERIFF REESE DROPPED ME OFF AS CLOSE TO MY office as the police tape would allow. I thanked him for the ride and was going to head straight to the office to work on the article with Zack, but I noticed two people standing around the crime scene so I went to them instead. As I got closer, I could barely believe my eyes. They were the farmers' ghosts, walking aimlessly in circles around where the coffins used to be. I glanced around and was relieved that there was nobody else around. The street felt empty and almost normal without the coffins there, the only thing marking this area as different was the police tape blocking traffic at either end of the block.

I walked up to the ghosts, and they both paused when they noticed I could see them.

"Hello," I said calmly, looking around at the

nearby shops to make sure none of the shopkeepers could see me talking to myself.

The man stared at me in silence, seemingly confused as to the whole situation.

"You can see us?" the woman asked.

I nodded. "I can, but most people won't be able to. My name is River."

"I'm Mary Littleton, and this is Frank. We own the farm just outside of Wells" she said as if striking up a polite conversation. Normalcy was good, and I tried my best to keep it up.

"It's very nice to meet you," I smiled. I wasn't too sure how to approach the situation, given that I didn't have any time to prepare.

Mrs. Littleton looked at me expectantly. I just stood there, smiling back awkwardly for a moment.

"Er…" I began. "Do you know why you're here?"

"Why yes," she said. "It appears we have been murdered." She smiled sweetly at me.

Again, I smiled back in silence. I was more than a little thrown off by how well she was handling this.

"Yes, you were." I noticed a pair of eyes staring out at me from the window of the sporting goods shop across the street.

I turned so my back was to the onlooker, then asked, "Do you both mind coming with me to my house?"

"How lovely," Mrs. Littleton said.

Mr. and Mrs. Littleton's ghosts followed me in silence as I walked home. I led them down to Mrs. Brody's apartment and introduced them to my pink-haired landlady.

"Lovely to meet you," Mrs. Brody said as we came into her kitchen.

I noticed a shocked-looking Mr. Richards floating behind her, and realized he was expecting to go on another search.

"We won't be needing help with the search," I said to him, apologizing when I noticed the disappointed look on his face. "They were waiting where the bodies were found."

He glanced back and forth at the two newcomers, made a *Hmph* noise, and then floated out of the room without saying a word.

"Sorry," I muttered under my breath. He had clearly been looking forward to the hunt.

"Oh never you mind him, dear," Mrs. Brody said to me, waving her hand in the direction Mr. Richards went. "Why don't you go upstairs and get the girls, I'll entertain our guests."

I glanced at Mr. And Mrs. Littleton, and they both smiled and nodded to me. This might be easier than I thought.

I stopped in my room on my way up to find the girls and was surprised to see Jessica standing next to the bed.

"Oh, hi," I said to her, pausing at the door. "I'm glad to see you didn't wander far. What are you doing in my room?"

She smiled at me. "I'm playing with your kitty." Soot was chasing her fingers as she waved her hand over my bed.

"He can see you?" I asked, astonished.

She nodded. "Well, yeah." She giggled and continued to play with the cat.

"Huh, cool." I watched the two interact with each other. I guess it made sense now why cats and witches were always assumed to go together in stories.

"There are people I would like you to meet," I said to her after a few minutes. "Can you come with me downstairs?"

She pouted.

"I can bring the cat," I added hastily. "Right, Soot?" The cat meowed.

Jessica beamed at me. "Okay. Yay!"

"Just one second, though, I need to grab the others." I left my room and ran up the stairs two at a time. The three girls were hanging out in the lounge and looked at me keenly as I came running up the stairs.

"Two more ghosts, can you guys come down?"

Bailey jumped up. "What? You're kidding. Two more?"

I nodded. "Yeah, unfortunately. An older couple.

They were found this morning. Same people that we saw in the fire."

The girls followed me down, and I picked Soot up on the way. Jessica followed us down into Mrs. Brody's apartment, and Soot jumped out of my arms as soon as we arrived and leaped towards his new friend as she followed me into the room.

I sat down at the kitchen table and addressed our new guests, "I don't mean to bring up bad memories, but do you remember anything about your murders?"

Mr. Littleton seemed mesmerized by Jessica and the cat and didn't seem to even notice I said anything.

Mrs. Littleton watched her husband momentarily with sad eyes, then turned her attention to me. "Of the murder, itself? No. But the last thing I remember was getting in our car to drive up to Brimstone Bay."

Well, that was interesting.

"Brimstone Bay?" I asked. "Why?"

"For the festival, of course."

"What if I told you that you were in Brimstone Bay right now?" Jane said as she joined us at the table.

The ghost looked at Jane in surprise and then turned back to me. "Are we? Oh, how lovely."

"So you were on your way here?" I asked. "Do you remember anything after getting in the car?"

She shook her head. "No, I just remember being

excited about the journey. We don't get out of the farm much these days."

I let out a loud sigh.

"I do," a small voice said from behind us.

I turned to see Jessica looking at us. "You do what?" I asked.

"I remember. We were driving," she said quietly. She closed her eyes, trying to remember. "We were coming to the festival, too."

I stared at her in disbelief. "Are you sure?"

She nodded. "We had never been before, and Mom promised that I could go see it. We left early, and I slept in the back."

"Do you remember anything else?" I asked, hoping for more.

She shook her head. "No, I just slept in the back. I couldn't remember before, but now I know that's the truth. I was sleeping in the back of the car, and then I was in the haunted house." She looked sad.

"It's okay, dear," Mrs. Littleton said, moving over to the girl. "There, there. No need to be sad. You did a good job in remembering."

Jessica smiled up at the woman in front of her, and I was glad to see how happy they looked together.

"So all of you were on your way here at the time of your murders," I said, mostly just thinking out loud to myself. "That can't be a coincidence."

"What are you going to do?" Bailey asked.

"Not sure yet. I've got to talk to the sheriff, though. Are you all okay here with the…" I paused, unsure what to call them. "Guests?" I finished.

"Of course we are," Mrs. Brody said. "Go, do your thing."

I went back up to my room to organize my thoughts before contacting the sheriff. I paced back and forth a few times, then decided it would be best to go see the mayor before talking to Sheriff Reese just so we would be on the same page before involving the police. I hoped he was feeling well enough to meet. Then I realized, I really didn't care. People are being murdered, and he would have to just suck it up.

I ran downstairs to grab my bike so I could get there faster, then sped into town as fast as I could on my rickety old thrift store bicycle.

The mayor's door was open, and the lights were on, so that was a good sign. I locked my bike to a bench and walked into his office. Only I was hit with what can only be explained as a concrete wall of exuding power. I had to stop and collect myself at the door before I could walk the rest of my way into his office.

Mayor Scott was sitting at his desk speaking with the vampire from the haunted house. The pale-faced man turned to look at me as I entered and bowed his head.

"Uh, hi Mayor Scott," I said awkwardly. "Nice to see you again."

He turned his attention back to the mayor. "That should be all for now, Mr. Mayor." He stood up and bowed, then walked out of the office without making eye contact with me.

As he left, the tension and level of power in the room subsided dramatically, and both Mayor Scott and I let out deep breaths.

"What's news, River?" He managed a small smile.

"Oh, you know. A whole lot right about now," I said.

The mayor laughed.

"Wow, that guy has a strong presence," I said as I approached the chair the vampire had been sitting in.

"That's an understatement," the mayor said. He looked much better than before and seemed to relax in his chair as I sat down. "Look, I wanted to talk to you about something. The sheriff filled me in this morning about the bodies. Two more symbols and two more sewn mouths. He also tells me, this time, the symbols were added after the people had been killed and that he thinks the killer might be getting sloppy."

I nodded and watched him thoughtfully.

"Whoever is doing this must obviously really have a thing against magic," he said. "Otherwise, they wouldn't have bothered with the symbols. If they're trying this hard to frame..." He paused, then continued, "...a certain community, then I don't doubt that they would go so far as to try and try and kill them, as well."

I leaned back in my chair and nodded. "I know."

"Just be careful, okay?"

I nodded, then we sat and just stared at each other for a long moment. Times were getting dark, and neither of us were prepared for what might come.

"So, what's news?" he asked me finally, breaking the silence.

"All three murder victims were heading to Brimstone Bay before they were murdered," I said. Right to the point. No sense beating around the bush.

"And should I ask how you know this?" he asked.

I shook my head. "Nope."

He nodded. "I see. Well, that's cause for concern. Do we know if they were murdered before they arrived, or after?"

"I have reason to believe they died before getting here." I wish I could tell him all the details about how I was getting this information, but while I definitely trusted him, I didn't know to what extent that trust could go. And given the secret of his that I discovered earlier today, I wasn't sure what other dark secrets he may be hiding.

Mayor Scott took in a deep breath and let it out dramatically. "We need to inform Sheriff Reese."

"I'll call him."

I unzipped my bag to grab my phone, but Mayor Scott interrupted. "No need. He's here." He tilted his chin in the direction of the door.

I turned to look, and Sheriff Reese came walking in. He sat down in the chair next to me without saying a word.

"Long day?" Mayor Scott asked him.

"You have no idea."

"Oh," the mayor answered. "I think I have some."

"Yeah, yeah, we've all had a long day," I said, feeling exasperated. I turned to look the sheriff in the eye. "Look, I have more information about the murders."

Sheriff Reese sat upright in his seat and looked at me.

"The victims were on their way here," I said. "On their way to Brimstone Bay."

"Are you serious? How do you know?" he asked.

I paused for a moment. "Facebook."

He nodded, clearly believing my reasoning. If there was one thing that Sheriff Reese didn't understand - apart from the paranormal, apparently - it was social media. I would have to keep that one in my arsenal for future use.

I glanced up at Mayor Scott who raised his eyebrows at me in reply. I shrugged.

"Whoever killed these people obviously knew they were coming this way, then," he said. "Do you think it has anything to do with the Shadow Festival? I've told the fair staff not to leave town, in case we need to question them further. You don't think it was one of them, do you?"

I shook my head. "Absolutely not. This is terribly bad for business. Murder would be the last thing anyone from the festival would want happening while they're in town. Right?"

"Mr. Kraevak, the festival director, was just in my office. He insisted his people have nothing to do with it, but they will cooperate fully with the investigation as it progresses."

"Do you believe him?" the sheriff asked.

"I do."

"I do, too," I added. Not that anyone asked me.

CHAPTER FIFTEEN

THE TOWN WAS ABSOLUTELY PACKED ON MY WALK into work the next day. The main street was nearly shoulder to shoulder people as I tried to weave my way through the crowd to get to my office. I practically had to shove my way to the door.

"What the hell is with all those people?" I asked JoAnn as I finally got to the office.

"Seems the murders have put Brimstone Bay on the map," she replied, putting aside the proof of this week's paper she had been reading.

"That's kind of gruesome," I said. I didn't realize murder made a place desirable.

She shrugged. "Seems death is good for business."

I put my bag down and went to look out the window. The streets were full of people, and the shops across the road were full. I noticed the

Shadow Festival decorations had been added too, and the entire street looked like a scene from a Halloween movie.

"Wow," I said, staring out at the scene below. "The festival must be doing really well." Seems I was wrong about murder being bad for the festival. The creepy vampire guy must be thrilled.

I pulled down the blinds to block out the view and set to work researching the murders.

I spent a solid few hours trying to see what more I could dig up on the symbols, but I was coming up blank. There had been no other instances of similar murders or anything else that involved the symbol in recent years. The only current article I could find on it was from a private museum's website, advertising an ancient dark magic exhibit that took place a few weeks ago.

I clicked on the article and scanned through the images. It seems the symbol was part of the exhibit. Interesting. I wondered if that was where the killer got his information from. I clicked on the website's *contact us* page button to see where the museum was located and was not really surprised to see it was located in Boston.

I sighed and sat back in my chair. I was finding it hard not to be suspicious of Ryan's new friends from Boston.

"I'm going to go look into something," I said to JoAnn, then left the office to go visit the coffee shop downstairs. I really needed to talk to Ryan's friends, unappealing as that idea was to me.

"Hi, Mr. Bramley," I said as I squeezed my way through the café to the back counter. This had to be the busiest I'd ever seen the place. I noticed he was working by himself behind the counter, frantically taking orders and pouring drinks. "Where's Ryan?"

"Fishing," he muttered, obviously not happy about it.

"I didn't know he fished," I commented.

"He doesn't. His friends do," he said. "Couldn't have picked a worse day to go."

"Is there anything I can help you with?" I asked.

He shook his head. "No thanks, River. But if you do see Ryan when he gets back, can you send him in here please?"

"Sure thing," I smiled, then waved goodbye and went to join the crowd in the street.

Wow, murder really was good for business. I couldn't get over the crowds that had gathered. There were line ups halfway down the block at the different food stands from the festival.

My phone buzzed, and I looked to see a text from Sheriff Reese saying he wants to meet at the mayor's office in 15 minutes.

I sighed. I don't know what these guys have against phone calls, but a simple call would eliminate the need to meet in person every ten minutes.

I slowly made my way down the street through the growing crowd of people. I caught the tail end of one couple's conversation as I walked past. The girl was asking her partner excitedly when he thought the next murder was going to take place. Man, people could be really twisted sometimes.

I finally made it to the mayor's office after zigzagging through the main street, dodging people like I was in some sort of zombie video game.

The sheriff was already in there waiting for me, both men sitting at the mayor's desk with large coffees in front of them. I was happy to see a third was waiting for me.

I sat down and graciously took my cup, ready for whatever information they had to throw at me.

"We've found another link between the two murders," Sheriff Reese said.

"We needed more stuff to link them together?" the mayor asked.

The sheriff ignored him. "We've determined the cause of death." He paused for dramatic effect.

"Well spit it out, then," Mayor Scott said, sounding quite agitated. The events of the past few days had taken a toll on all of us.

"All three victims died of heart attacks."

"What?" I said, shocked. "How does a thirteen-year-old girl die from a heart attack?"

"The autopsies revealed all three victims has traces of a very strong paralytic in their systems. We suspect they ingested it through inhalation. My guess is that they overdosed on the drug," he explained. "The exact nature of the paralytic hasn't been determined yet. It's nothing we've seen before – nothing chemical. We've sent samples off to Boston for further testing."

"Why would the killer want to paralyze them?" Mayor Scott asked.

"To carve the symbols into their skin," I suggested. I then shuddered. "Would they still have been able to feel it?"

The sheriff shrugged. "The two older victims sure didn't. But why would someone want to put that mark on an already dead body is beyond me."

I shook my head, trying to make sense of it all.

After a few moments of silence, the sheriff asked, "What should we do with all those people outside?"

"Let them snoop," the mayor suggested. "Brimstone Bay sure needs the economic boost these people are bringing. If it becomes a problem for the investigation, we can do what we can to make them leave. In the meantime, I suggest we let them stay."

"So long as another body doesn't show up, that's fine by me," Sheriff Reese answered.

"My story is due tomorrow," I said. "How much of this should I reveal in the paper?"

"Still leave out the details, if you can," the

sheriff said. "Cases like this often promote copycats, and we want to prevent that as best we can."

I nodded. "Okay then, just the basics. No problem." So much for world-class journalism.

I spotted the creepy vampire guy lurking around the corner when I left the mayor's office. I decided to go speak with him, curious to see if there was anything else said during his meeting with the mayor that Mayor Scott didn't tell me. He was looking rather pleased, looking out over the crowd.

I pushed my way through the crowd, and he turned his face slowly to look at me as I approached. It was really creepy the way he did that.

"Ms. Halloway," he said to me, bowing his head. I noticed his power wasn't so overwhelming standing outside in the open. Thank God for that.

"You look happy," I said. He looked down at me and frowned. "Er... Mr. Kraevak." I said quickly. I got the impression that he was used to people treating him with the highest of respect.

"In the line of work I am in, Ms. Halloway, you find that dark happenings are good for business."

"Murder, you mean," I said.

He nodded. "Yes, murder."

"And did you know this beforehand?" I asked, trying to make out the expression on his stone-still face.

"You get to know a lot of things when you grow to be my age."

He looked me up and down, his eyes lingering on my shirt. I instinctively looked down at myself as well and guessed he wasn't impressed with my torn baggy jeans and AC/DC t-shirt. It's been a long couple of days, and I decided to dress comfy and casual today. So sue me.

I narrowed my eyes. "Did you have anything to do with the murders, Mr. Kraevak?" I figured I might as well ask.

His face remained expressionless. "Don't be absurd," he said, then walked out into the crowd and disappeared. I wondered how he was managing to be outside in broad daylight. Weren't Vampires supposed to burst into flames by the sun? I laughed at myself at the thought, knowing first-hand that you can't believe every paranormal myth you hear. Being a witch, you would have thought I would know better than to assume.

I noticed my legs were shaking, and didn't realize how utterly intimidated I had been by that man. I took a few deep breaths to steady myself, then made my way back to the office, away from the crowd and creepy, powerful men.

I had a lot of work to do and locked myself in my office for the entirety of the afternoon so I could concentrate on my work. I did my best to ignore Zack, who was sitting at JoAnn's desk typing away at his laptop. We were supposed to be working together, but I worked way better when I could focus on my own thoughts for a while. Luckily, he was the same, and we allowed each other to go about our own business.

I must have lost track of time because before I knew it the sky had grown dark, and the noise from the crowd outside had died town. I checked the clock on my laptop, and it was nearly midnight. Wow, I really must have been focused on my work.

My eyes were burning from staring at my computer for so long, and I really needed to get home to get some sleep. I packed up my bag and said goodbye to Zack, then headed down the now quiet main street, feeling rather like a zombie. I was grateful that the crowd had dispersed, as I really just wanted to get home quickly to sleep. I walked the few blocks to the mayor's office to grab my bike and walked it down the main street towards home, too tired to even attempt to balance on that thing.

I turned the corner and nearly had a heart attack as I walked straight into somebody walking towards me.

"Jesus Christ," I said, holding my hand over my heart, which was beating a thousand miles a minute.

"Wow, sorry about that," a low voice said. "Good timing there, River."

I glanced up to see Jordan standing in front of me in the shadows.

I tried to regain my breath. "Jordan, you scared

me." My heart was still pounding, but I relaxed a little bit. "What are you doing out this late?" I asked.

"Just out for a walk," he said.

I looked around, the street was deserted. He watched me curiously.

"This late at night?" That seemed suspicious.

He shrugged. "It's a nice night."

I noticed he was doing something with his hands, but I couldn't tell what through the darkness. I took a few steps sideways into the light of a street lamp, hoping he would follow. He didn't, which made it even harder for me to see him in the shadows now that I was in the light. I sighed and stepped back into the darkness, all the while Jordan was watching me.

"What are you doing out this late?" he asked.

"Just heading home from work." I reached for my phone and swiped the screen on, shining the light from my phone on him so I could see him better.

He was winding a spool of fishing line.

"What are you doing with that?" I asked. I could feel my face go cold, and I took a step back from him, trying to shake the images of the three corpses with their sewn mouths out of my head.

He noticed me step away, then immediately put the fishing line in his pocket.

"Nothing," he said.

"No really, what are you doing with that?" I felt

the instinct to run, but my feet were frozen to the ground.

"Relax, we just went fishing. What do you think?" he eyed me up and down.

"A bit late to be fishing," I said.

He shrugged. "We've been back a while. The fish weren't biting."

I nodded slowly. "Well, that's a shame." I swallowed, trying to maintain an even voice.

"Can I walk you home?" he asked. "It's late, and you shouldn't be out walking alone. What with the murders, and all."

"Yeah, I guess not," I managed to say. "But I'm alright, I live close, and my housemates are expecting me any minute," I lied.

"You sure?"

I nodded. "Yeah, honestly. I'm fine."

His phone buzzed then, and he glanced down at his screen.

"Shit, I gotta go," he said quickly. "Be safe."

He slid his phone into his back pocket and jogged off down the main street. I watched him leave and felt my body relax a bit.

I looked around to make sure I was alone, then, with my newfound energy, hopped on my bike and rode off in the direction of home. I kept my phone handy in my back pocket, in the event I needed to call for help. I didn't know whether the thought comforted or scared me.

It didn't take long before I got to my room, and threw myself on the bed in exhaustion. The house was unnaturally quiet for this time of night. The girls often stayed up late watching movies and messing around upstairs. How nice it must be to not have to work.

I closed my eyes and nearly dozed off when my phone rang loudly next to my ear.

I groaned and saw that Bailey was calling.

"Yes?" I said, my voice lazy with sleep.

"River," Bailey sounded frantic. "We need you to come to the station. Mrs. Brody has been arrested."

CHAPTER SIXTEEN

"MRS. BRODY WAS WHAT?" I SAT BOLT UPRIGHT IN bed, my body suddenly alert with adrenaline.

"Arrested. They think she had something to do with the murders," Bailey said desperately into the phone. "Please just get here. We can't make Sheriff Reese see reason."

"I'll be right there."

I leaped out of bed in a panic and grabbed my phone and a black hoodie that I had left on the floor. I then ran down the stairs to the back yard to grab my bike while clumsily trying to pull my hoodie over my head.

The small police station was just outside of town, and I cycled hard to get there as fast as I could. The night had gotten cold, and I put up my hood to stay warm from the cold wind that blew over my face as I sped down the road on my bike. I dumped my bike at the front door, and locked it up to a street sign as I heard a number of raised voices all shouting over each other coming from inside the station. Unable to figure out the damn lock in my panic, I dropped by bike and ran into the station to see what the heck was going on.

Rory screamed as I ran into the station, and all voices went quiet. I paused, looking frantically from one person to the next. All eyes were on Rory, who had her hand on her chest, staring at me. She looked pale.

"What's going on?" I demanded.

"Jesus Christ, River," Rory said, collapsing in a heap on a nearby chair.

"What?" I asked again. By the looks on everyone else's faces, no one else knew why she had screamed.

"Look at yourself," she said to me, then stood up and dragged me to the back end of the room to look in a mirror on the wall.

I stared at my reflection and felt my skin grow cold. Bailey and Jane came to stand with us and watched my reflection in the mirror as well.

"Holy crap," I said, taking in the view of my ratty-looking likeness staring back at me. Black shoes, torn baggy jeans, a black hoodie…

"We didn't see the killer in the fire," Rory whispered. "We were seeing the next victim."

I stepped away from the mirror, and immediately tore off the hoodie.

"That could just be a coincidence," I said, desperately trying to reassure myself. My reflection did look exactly like the image we saw in the flames a few nights ago.

"No such thing as coincidence, dears," Mrs. Brody said from across the room. I looked over to her to see the small, pink-haired woman was handcuffed to her chair. Her hair was disheveled, and she was wearing a pink ruffled nightgown. It was quite the scene.

"What are you talking about?" Sheriff Reese asked her, putting his hand on her shoulder.

"Get your wandering hands off me, you little perv," she snapped at him. He immediately recoiled his hands as if she had bit him.

I shook my head to clear my thoughts, trying to forget what I had just seen in the mirror.

"What's going on here? What the hell did you do?" I asked the sheriff, staring angrily at him.

Mayor Scott came striding into the room. "It's not his fault. I brought her in."

I turned to him. "You what?' I demanded. "Explain."

He sighed, his eyes looked tired, and he sat down in one of the nearby chairs.

The girls were staring at him angrily, crossing their arms and tapping their feet anxiously.

"After the paralytic was found in the victims, I didn't have much of a choice," he said.

I looked back and forth from him to Mrs. Brody. She rolled her eyes at him.

"I'm not following," I said.

"She doesn't exactly have the cleanest reputation," he said. "She poisoned all those people at the bake sale years ago."

It was my turn to roll my eyes. "Don't be ridiculous."

"She had nothing to do with that," Rory said, staring daggers at the man.

"I thought that was a school group rehearsing some kind of play," the sheriff said.

Now Mayor Scott rolled his eyes.

"I'm not stupid," he said to Rory. "I know exactly what happened, and how."

"What happened?" the sheriff asked.

"Never you mind your nosy little nose," Mrs. Brody snapped at him, making him jump again.

"Did your boys find anything?" the mayor asked, turning his attention to Sheriff Reese.

"Nothing but a few weird cooking herbs," he answered. "Nothing by the name of devil's flower or whatever."

"Devil's root," the mayor said.

Bailey's eyes went wide, and she exchanged a worried look with Rory.

"You searched her apartment?" I asked, shocked. "Do you have a warrant?"

"Don't be ridiculous," Sheriff Reese said to me, his voice even. "We just took a friendly look around. She didn't mind."

"The hell I didn't mind," Mrs. Brody snapped. "Rummaging through a defenseless old lady's things."

Sheriff Reese patted her shoulder trying to calm her, to which she responded with an attempt to bite his fingers. He pulled his hand away quickly, then put it in his pocket so he wouldn't make that mistake again.

"What's devil's root?" I asked the mayor, trying my best to sound innocent.

"Don't play dumb, River," he said to me, narrowing his eyes.

I looked at Mrs. Brody, who was staring down at her feet. The mayor was right; she didn't have the cleanest reputation. But I seriously doubted Mrs. Brody to be capable of anything as serious as a murder. However, the memory of smelling boiling devil's root during bridge night gnawed at my thoughts, and I had only really known the woman for a few months. I had absolutely no idea how Mayor Scott knew about devil's root, though.

"We didn't find any of it, whatever it was," Sheriff Reese repeated to the Mayor.

Mayor Scott nodded. "Okay, fair enough. I just had to do my due diligence. You can let her go."

"Seems you're innocent, Mrs. Brody," the sheriff said to her as he unlocked her handcuffs.

"Of course I'm innocent, you big buffoon," she spat at him. "Next time pick on someone your own size."

"I'm sorry," he muttered to her. I didn't realize what an influence she had on the sheriff. I wondered what their back story was. I tried to hide the smirk that was forming on my lips.

"Now that this embarrassment of a circus is over, we need to get home," Bailey said. "We have more important things to worry about."

"More important than a murder investigation?" Sheriff Reese chided her.

She glared at him, then reached for my hand and pulled me towards the front door.

"I expect you'll be giving us a ride home?" she said back to the sheriff, her voice short.

"Yeah, sure," he said. "Car's out back. I'll pull it around."

I sat down next to Mayor Scott and raised my eyebrow at him, hoping for further explanation.

"Don't look at me that way, River," he said. "You know it's my duty to protect this town. It's our job to bring in suspects, however unlikely they may seem."

"Yeah but you know Mrs. Brody isn't capable of anything like this," I said.

He sighed. "I know, but you can't be too careful."

A honk came from outside, and we went outside to see two cop cars waiting for us. I locked my bike up, my hands a lot steadier now than they were before, and got in the second car with Officer George, one of the local policemen. We rode home in silence, and I was thankful for the few peaceful minutes I had before arriving back at home.

I thanked him as he dropped me off, and caught the tail end of Mrs. Brody shouting at Sheriff Reese as I got out of the car behind them.

"Oh, stuff it, pretty boy," she said, slamming the car door shut. I offered a small smile to the defeated looking sheriff as he drove by, and he gave me a little wave in response.

I let out a loud sigh. This day couldn't possibly get any longer.

I followed the girls down into Mrs. Brody's apartment, and she made us a pot of tea as we sat around the kitchen table.

"You okay, Mrs. Brody?" I asked her as she poured me a cup.

"Oh yes, dear," she said. "Of course. I just like to keep those boys on their toes."

I laughed. "I think Sheriff Reese is terrified of you."

"And he should be," she said. "I used to look after him as a young boy, and the stories I could tell you about him would make him red in the ears."

"How didn't they find the devil's root?" Bailey asked.

Mrs. Brody joined us around the kitchen table and sighed. "My entire stash went missing the other morning. I figured one of you lot had borrowed it."

I glanced around at the girls. "Did you?"

They all shook their heads.

"So someone stole your devil's root?" Jane asked. "Why?"

"I don't know, but I doubt it's for anything good," she said.

"Mayor Scott said there was a paralytic found in the bodies," Bailey said. "I wonder if it was the devil's root."

"Could be," I offered. "But the victims weren't killed here, we don't think. They were killed in different cities, then brought here later. It makes it seem unlikely."

Unlikely, but possible. As Mrs. Brody says, there is no such thing as a coincidence.

"Are you sure someone stole it, Mrs. Brody?" Rory said, speaking slowly and trying to choose her words carefully. "You didn't accidentally mix up your herbs again, did you? You can be honest."

"Don't be bloody ridiculous, child," she snapped at Rory. "Absolutely not."

"I'm sorry, I just wanted to be sure," Rory apologized.

"Off to bed with all of you," Mrs. Brody instructed us. "And River, dear, sleep in one of the girls' rooms tonight, just to be safe."

"Sure thing, Mrs. Brody."

Soot was waiting for us up in the third-floor lounge room, accompanied by Jessica and Mr. and Mrs. Littleton.

"Oh hello," Mrs. Littleton cooed sweetly to us as we arrived in the lounge. "What a lovely place you have here."

It was already two o'clock in the morning, but there was no way I could sleep now. I lay back on the couch, rubbing my temples with my fingers, eyes tightly shut.

"You look terrible," Jessica said.

"Thanks," I said. "I don't exactly feel like a million bucks."

We all chatted for a while about the events of the evening. Jane was curious as to why I wasn't home when the arrest went down, and I explained I had lost track of time at work. I then told her I ran into Jordan, and that seemed to pique everyone's interest.

"Is that one of Ryan's friends?" Jane asked.

I nodded. "Yeah, from Boston. Came up for the festival."

"You ran into him in the street at midnight?" Rory asked. "What was he doing out that late?"

"I don't know," I admitted. "I was wondering the same myself."

"Is he the hot blond one?" Jane asked.

Rory nodded. "Yeah, the one with the dreamy blue eyes."

"He asked me out for coffee." I'm unsure why I let that spill out.

"Are you going out with him?" Bailey asked, sitting up straight. She knew Ryan was interested in me, and I had a feeling deep down she was jealous about that.

I shrugged. "Too busy to think about that sort of thing right now."

A tight knot was beginning to form in my stomach, and I didn't have the heart to tell them I suspected he might have something to do with the murders. I couldn't get the image of him winding the fishing line out of my mind.

"River, you're as pale as a ghost," Bailey now looked concerned.

"Hey," Jessica said. "Not nice."

Bailey ignored her. "Seriously," she said to me. "What's going on?"

I shook my head. "Nothing. I just think we should stay away from Ryan's friends. I don't trust them."

"Er, okay," Rory sounded hesitant. "What is it that you're not telling us?"

"Honestly, nothing," I lied. "I'm just a bit rattled

by today, that's all. The whole hooded image thing threw me off a bit."

Jessica came to stand next to me. "Are you talking about my killer?"

I glanced up at her. "I'm not so sure that was your killer."

"What do you mean?" she said, sounding defensive. "I'm sure that was him."

"How do you know it was him? We couldn't see the person's face in the flames," I said.

"I just know," she said indignantly.

"Come to think of it," Mrs. Littleton said quietly from behind us. "I do remember a young man walking through the fields earlier in the day, before leaving for Brimstone Bay."

I sat bolt upright. "Do you actually?"

She nodded. "It wasn't out of the norm, though. People often cut through our farm to get to the town."

"Could you see what he looked like?" Jane asked.

Mrs. Littleton shook her head. "I wasn't wearing my glasses. I think he was wearing a hooded jacket, though. I couldn't see his face."

I collapsed back on the couch and looked around at my housemates.

"So, now what? How do we figure out who we saw in the flames?" I asked.

"I don't know, but I think it's safe to say you shouldn't wear that outfit ever again," Rory said.

"As if eliminating an outfit will prevent a prophecy from coming true," I said.

"It's a magic prophecy, River," Bailey said. "You never know what it means until it happens."

I rubbed my eyes, the weight of the day's events finally crashing down on me, hard.

"I need to sleep," I said. "Can we finish this over breakfast?"

I yawned and closed my eyes, and drifted off to sleep on the couch.

CHAPTER SEVENTEEN

I WOKE UP TO A LOUD BANGING NOISE IN THE morning and jumped up in panic.

"What's going on?" I asked sleepily. My shoulders popped as I stretched, and I was stiff from sleeping awkwardly on the couch. Soot had curled up on my legs, and I scratched his ears as he purred against me.

Bailey was awake, standing next to one of the small windows facing the front yard.

"Mrs. Brody is throwing things at people in front of the house," she sounded incredulous, as if she didn't believe what she was saying.

"What?" I got up to see what she was talking about.

Mrs. Brody was outside in her same pink nightgown, picking up twigs from the lawn and throwing them at the crowd of people who had gathered in front of the house.

"What the hell is she doing?" I asked.

"I don't know, but I think she's finally lost it."

"What's happening?" A tired-sounding Rory emerged from her bedroom. "What happened?" she repeated, yawning audibly.

"Mrs. Brody is putting on a show," I said.

Jane then came out of her room and joined us all at the front window. We watched Mrs. Brody shouting and waving the crowd away for a few minutes, throwing clumps of dirt and plants at them from the front yard. A few people had their cameras out and were taking pictures. That seemed to aggravate her even more, and she picked up a small rock and threw it at one of the camera-wielding onlookers. Luckily she missed.

"We had better go down and see what's going on," Rory said.

"Man, too bad I have to live with her," I laughed. "This would make a great story for the paper."

"Crazy pink-haired lady attacks tourists with garden trimmings," Jane laughed.

I was the only one fully dressed, still wearing last night's clothes, so I went down to see what was going on while the others got dressed.

"Mrs. Brody," I called from the front door. "Could you please come here for a moment."

I could hear her make a *hmph* noise, but she

dropped her sticks and stormed back to the house.

I raised my eyebrow curiously at her as she stomped up the stairs, her cheeks smudged with dirt from the garden. I suppressed a laugh as best I could, so as to not piss her off any more than she already seemed to be.

"Seems word got out that I was arrested last night," she cried, her voice shrill with annoyance. "Everybody wants to come see the little old lady who got away with murder."

"Seriously?" I asked. "How did they find out this is where you live?"

She shrugged. "Someone must have seen the police cars come around last night."

"Either way," I said. "We've got protective spells around the property, remember? No one can get past the property line that we don't know."

"Yes, yes," she said, tossing the clumps of garden trimmings aside that she still had in her hands. She wiped her filthy hands on her nightgown and then sighed loudly, looking back at the crowd standing on the sidewalk.

"Let's have breakfast, shall we?" I asked. "We could all use some down time."

"Fine, but don't think I'm cooking a big meal for you lot," she snapped at me, then led the way into the house.

The girls joined us downstairs in Mrs. Brody's kitchen not long after, accompanied by Mr. and Mrs.

Littleton and Jessica, followed not far behind by Soot.

I started digging through the cabinets looking for something to cook but was quickly ushered away by an exasperated Mrs. Brody.

"Oh, shoo," she said, waving me away with a dirty hand. "I've got this. Sit down, dear."

After a few minutes, the kitchen became very crowded as Mr. Richards and a few of his friends showed up. I guess it didn't take long for word to spread about there being new ghosts in town, and the crowd outside must have sparked a few questions.

"Busy day you're having," one of the new ghosts said conversationally. "Well, well, who have we here?"

He approached Mr. and Mrs. Littleton and introduced himself, "Gary Rotterdam, a pleasure to make your acquaintance."

The ghosts started chatting amongst themselves and moved to the living room, graciously giving us space.

"You look absolutely appalling," Mr. Richards said to Mrs. Brody. "What on earth have you done with yourself?"

Mrs. Brody didn't answer but waved her hand in the general direction of the front of the house as she continued preparing breakfast. The smell of pancakes started wafting from the oven, and my stomach made a grumbling noise.

"I'll make coffee," I offered, and got up go busy myself with the task.

"Apparently, there are new ghosts in town," Mr. Richards said conversationally to the room.

I turned to face him. "What do you mean? How new?"

"Newer than these three," he said, motioning towards the living room.

"Where?"

"Where else? The haunted house."

I eyed him suspiciously, unsure if he was being truthful or simply stirring the pot.

I then made up my mind. "I have to go see."

"Not this instant, missy," Mrs. Brody said, waving her finger at me. "First, you eat, then you go play with ghosts."

I sighed. "Fine, but only because I'm starving."

I devoured breakfast, eager to go to the haunted house for a visit. I hadn't heard word of another murder, so I suspected Mr. Richards was either messing with us for the hell of it or maybe just talking about the ghosts who I had initially seen at the haunted house when it first opened. My guess was the latter, but you couldn't be too sure.

"Thanks so much for the breakfast, Mrs. Brody," I said, wiping syrup from my lips. "Sorry to eat and run."

"We're coming with you," Bailey said, and she

and the girls quickly finished their plates and moved to follow me.

"I'm fine on my own," I said, really preferring to go investigate by myself.

"Not after seeing you as a victim last night, River," Bailey said. "Until the killer is caught, you don't get the luxury of being alone."

Dammit, I wasn't going to get any peace until this whole thing was over.

"Alright well, let's get this thing figured out then," I said.

"I'll drive," Rory offered. She was the only one with a car, and I was grateful that we wouldn't have to walk through town with all the tourists.

Luckily we found parking nearby, and we only had to walk a block to the haunted house. A crowd had gathered around it, and I saw a few familiar faces nearby.

"Dammit," I muttered under my breath.

"Hi River," an eager voice called from behind the crowd. Roger came running up to us, a broad smile on his face.

"I thought you had gone back home," I said to him.

He shook his head. "Nope, not until next week."

Great, just what I needed. More company.

"Hi River," I heard another voice call out.

"Seriously?"

Ryan and his friends were walking towards us,

and I noticed Bailey had a giant smile on her face.

"Hi Ryan," she said as they approached.

"Hey Bailey," he said to her, then turned his attention back to me. "What are you guys doing here?"

"I could ask you the same question."

"Just checking out the house," he said. "It's become a bit of a hot spot since the murder."

"I can see that," I looked around at the growing crowd, then glanced back at Bailey and the girls. We had no hope of looking for ghosts through this crowd.

"They even put the coffins back that the other bodies were found in," Roger said eagerly.

"You're kidding," I said. I couldn't believe that. But then again, if it was good for business…

"Well, we're not staying," I said. "We were actually just passing by."

"Great, us too," Jordan said. "Why don't we all grab a coffee?"

"That sounds great," Bailey said quickly before I had a chance to refuse the invitation. "We could all use a coffee, I'm sure."

I shot her a stink eye, but she didn't notice.

"I've gotta get back," Roger said to no one in particular. "My aunt will be expecting me."

"Okay Roger, see you later," I said to him, as he ran off. At least that's one less person to deal with.

The seven of us walked off together towards the

café, Bailey trying to strike up a conversation with Ryan the whole way. The poor girl was met with one-word answers, but to her credit she pushed on, trying desperately to keep the conversation alive.

"Why were you guys lurking around the haunted house?" I asked Jordan as he walked up next to me. "You've seen it before, nothing new there."

He shrugged. "No, but it seems more interesting now that everyone else is interested in it."

I raised my eyebrow. "That's stupid."

He shrugged again.

I really didn't trust the guy, but felt comfortable enough with him in a public place surrounded by people I knew. Still, I tried to keep my distance.

We walked past the two coffins that had been returned.

"I can't believe they actually put the coffins back," Bailey said to Ryan. "Why do you think they did that?"

"Dunno," Ryan said quietly, refusing to even look in the direction of the coffins. Man, the poor girl was drowning.

The café was packed, but Ryan led us into the back room that they reserved for special occasions. "I'll bring us some coffees." He left to go help his dad at the front counter.

"The cops any closer to solving the murder?" Jordan asked me as we all sat down around a long table.

"How would I know?" I shrugged my shoulders noncommittally.

"I've seen you with the sheriff," he responded. "I assumed you were involved in it."

He seemed far too interested in this for my liking and asked far too many questions.

"Just for the paper."

Rory recognized that I really wasn't having a good time talking to the guy, so she stepped in and started asking questions about Boston. Bless her, she always knew how to act in situations like this. I was hopeless when it came to this sort of thing.

Ryan came back a while later with a tray of coffees and sat them down in front of us.

"And a Triple Americano, black, for the girl who hates lattes," he said to me as he passed me my coffee.

I could feel Jordan's eyes on me, but I very intently refused to meet his gaze. I gave Ryan a chastising look but then muttered a "thank you" for my coffee.

I knew for a fact he just said that because he saw Jordan and me having coffee together the other day.

Ryan pulled up a chair and sat at the far end of the room, facing us.

"Scared we'll bite?" I said to him, laughing.

"Just want to be ready if my dad needs me," he mumbled.

"So guys, when do you head back to Boston?" Rory asked, drawing the attention away from Ryan.

"Probably this weekend," Jordan said. "But not confirmed yet."

He glanced at his friend who grunted and looked away.

"Not much of a talker, are ya?" I said to him. He ignored me, and I rolled my eyes. This guy was a class-A douche bag if I did say so myself.

"So who do you guys think did it?" Jordan asked, bringing the conversation back to the murders. "What kind of person would carve a pagan symbol into a dead body?"

I really wanted to know why he was so obsessed with this murder.

"Witches," Ryan spat.

I raised my eyebrows at him. "Witches? Really?" I laughed at him, and his face turned a brilliant shade of red. He stared down at his feet and sipped his coffee, shrugging at me. "Didn't think you believed in that stuff."

He shrugged. "Who else would do such a thing? It's dark and gruesome, no regular person would do something like this."

"Come on man," Jordan said. "Probably just some prankster asshole trying to make a name for himself as some sort of pagan serial killer. Bastard probably wants a movie made after him."

"He'll probably get one," Rory said. "Or she."

"That's the last thing we need," I said. I eyed Ryan as he sipped his coffee. I didn't realize the murders had gotten to him so much.

"You didn't know the victims, did you?" I asked Ryan, curious if that's why he was so upset over this.

He shook his head. "No, it's just that I find it terrifying. Who knows what dark magic is out there. We should all be careful."

Both of his friends laughed at him at that point.

"Dude, don't be ridiculous," Jordan said. "I think the festival has gotten to your head."

He shrugged. "Maybe."

"How does anyone catch a murderer, anyway? There's an entire world they could be hiding in, it's like finding a needle in a haystack" Jordan asked me, really not wanting to let this topic go.

"You're right, and often they don't get found," I said. "But I suppose, to start you would retrace their steps. Follow the sites of the murders, that sort of thing, and hope that the murderer left something behind."

Ryan was fidgeting with his coffee lid. "You watch too much CSI."

"Yeah, maybe," I offered. "But if there's one thing you learn from those shows, is that everybody makes mistakes."

"Why don't we change the subject," Bailey suggested, recognizing Ryan's discomfort.

The topic was switched to baseball, something I

was so absolutely not interested in.

The amount of work I had to do started nagging the back of my mind, and I felt I really should leave to prepare my articles for the week. I've really enjoyed the excuses not to coop myself up in the office with Zack, but the idea of staying down here with these two guys appealed to me even less. Sure, Jordan was deliriously good-looking and seemed to like me, unlike Zack who was an arrogant asshole who treated me like a petulant little child, but at the moment my job and Zack won out.

I looked at my phone then said, "Look, guys, I really should get to the office. I have lots of work to do."

Bailey smiled. "Okay, don't work too hard. Call me when you're done, and we'll walk home together."

"Sure thing," I said. "Thanks for the coffee, Ryan."

"Ryan, why don't you come sit here," Bailey said as I cleared the seat next to her.

"Can't, gotta help my dad." He then walked out of the room without saying another word.

Bailey raised her eyebrow at me, and I shrugged in response, then waved goodbye to the rest of the group.

"Hope to see you soon," Jordan said to me.

I pretended not to hear him as I walked out of the café.

CHAPTER EIGHTEEN

LATER THAT NIGHT THE GIRLS AND I WERE HANGING out on the back porch. It was a warm evening, and we wanted to enjoy the beautiful weather while we could. Soon it would be too cold to hang out outside, and we would be cooped up in the house all winter.

"You know, we really need to solve this case before the entire town believes they were murdered by witches," I said, staring off into the bay on the other side of our back yard. It really was a beautiful view, and it had been a solid week since I had enough time to go for a run. I really missed the waterfront.

"Do you think it could actually have been witches?" Jane asked.

I shook my head. "No, I really don't think so. It just doesn't make sense."

"Well whoever it is, I really hope they get caught

soon. I don't know how much longer I can live on edge like this," Rory said. "Knowing any one of us could be next, it just freaks me out. I can't sleep."

"We just really need Jessica and Mr. and Mrs. Littleton to remember more about their murders," I said. I had no idea how we were going to manage that, given the fact that none of them seemed to remember anything from the actual events.

"You could try bringing the ghosts back to where they were murdered," Bailey suggested.

"Not really, because we don't know exactly where they happened," I said. "They were driving on their way here, and there's no way we will be able to get them to their vehicles without raising suspicion."

"What about bringing them back to where their bodies were left?" Rory asked. "The killer would have obviously been there with them. Maybe their ghosts were there as well, they just don't remember because they were so new."

"That's actually an excellent idea," I said. "Do any of you know how long it takes for a person to come back as a spirit after they die?"

"No idea, but I know someone who would," Rory said, pulling herself out of the hammock hanging from the porch above. "Let's go inside."

Mrs. Brody was busy fussing with her plants when we came in, and Jessica and Mr. and Mrs. Littleton were chatting around her kitchen table.

"Mrs. Brody, how much do you know about ghosts?" Rory asked.

"Oh, more than I care to know, dear."

"Hey," Jessica said to her. "That's not nice."

We all ignored her.

"How long does it take for one to appear after their bodies are killed?" I asked.

She paused and thought for a moment. "Oh, instantly, I would imagine."

Rory and I exchanged looks.

"Why on earth would you need to know that?" she asked us.

"We're trying to find a way to trigger the memories of the murder victims," I said. "We need to find their killer before someone else is murdered, and I have a feeling we're running out of time."

"You girls aren't going to the crime sites, are you?" She looked sternly at us and crossed her arms.

"We don't have a choice," I said. "If we're going to prevent anyone else from succumbing to the same fate as Jessica and Mr. and Mrs. Littleton, we need to do something drastic to jog their memories."

"I'm coming with you," she then said to us.

"Nuh-huh," I said. "No way. You're already implicated enough in this. If the mayor catches you lurking about the crime scene, we'll have a really hard time convincing him of your innocence."

"Well, that's just too bad."

Rory sighed. "I wouldn't fight it, River. When she makes up her mind, that's the end of the story."

I shook my head in disbelief. "Fine, but if we get caught and you end up in jail, don't say I didn't warn you."

"Don't be silly," she said. "Besides, I'm the only one who knows the resident ghosts."

Huh, I guess she had a point.

"We need a cover story," Rory said as we prepared to leave. "In case we are caught in the house. What are we going to say?"

"I think it's best to just tell the truth," I said. "That I thought we could find out more information at the scene of the crime, and you all wanted to come to protect me."

Rory shrugged. "It's as good a story as any. A non-story, rather."

"Do we really have to go back to that place?" Jessica asked.

I nodded. "Yeah, I'm so sorry. It's the only way to try and trigger your memory. We can try the same with the coffins, but as they're out in public, it might be harder to go without people seeing us."

"Okay fine," she said. "Want us to meet you there?"

"That would be best. We'll be there in 15 minutes."

Mrs. Brody led us through her apartment to Rory's car parked in the front driveway, but we all crashed into her awkwardly as she froze at the front door.

"What's going on?" I asked her.

She stayed silent, and I pushed passed her to see what the problem was.

"Oh crap," I said. The girls pushed through to see for themselves.

The grass has been torn up, large circles formed in the front lawn. At first, it looked like some sort of crop circles, but it quickly dawned on me what it was.

"It's the symbol," Rory said, her voice wavering with fear. The curse mark had been carved into the grass.

"It really was you we saw in the fire, River," Jane said, stepping forward to grab my hand.

I swallowed hard, trying to will myself to speak, but my body seemed frozen in place.

"Prophecies can be changed," Mrs. Brody said. "And we will change this one."

I nodded. "Okay, yeah. Let's do that, please."

We all looked around the lawn quickly to make sure no one was here. It was more of an instinctual response to the situation than a necessity, as our magic could sense that there was no one else on the property at the moment. I had no idea why Mrs. Brody's protective spells didn't prevent this from happening. I really didn't want to know what sort of trick would have gotten through.

"Quick, to the car," Mrs. Brody said, leading the way to Rory's car. Her voice was wavering, and I could tell she was just as concerned about the trespass as I was.

We all got in the car quickly, and Rory locked the doors.

"Okay, which way should we go?" Rory asked, pulling out of the driveway.

"Avoid the main street," I said. "Maybe park where we did earlier today."

It only took us a few minutes to arrive, and we all sat in the dark car for a few moments, scoping out our surroundings.

"Shit," I said. "Is that Mayor Scott?" I squinted to try and see better, but I was pretty sure that's who I saw walking around near the haunted house a few blocks ahead.

"Yeah, that's definitely him," Bailey said. "What are we going to do?"

"I'll take care of him," Mrs. Brody said. "You girls wait ten minutes before going into the house, okay? Be careful. Oh, and say hello to Buella for me."

She then got out of the car and marched down the center of the road towards Mayor Scott.

"What do you think she's up to?" I asked.

Rory shrugged. "No one ever knows but her."

"And who's Buella?" Jane asked.

I shrugged.

We watched as the two chatted for a bit outside, then he led her away down the street with his arm wrapped around her. Ah, she pulled the frail old lady card. Nice.

We waited a few minutes until we knew the coast was clear, and then quietly got out of the car, careful to make as little noise as possible. We then walked the other way down the block and approached the house through the back lane.

It was a clear night, and the stars provided enough light for us to see. But if the way was clear enough for us to see, then it meant other people could see us as well. We crouched down low and walked along the back fence, so hopefully, no one would be able to see us walk up to the back of the house.

I pointed to the cellar door, remembering how Ryan and his friends had said that's how they had gotten into the house on its opening day. Luckily, the latched door was still unlocked, and we quietly made our way in through the small, dark cellar into the main house.

We paused and waited for a few minutes after entering, listening carefully to hear if there was anyone else around.

Jessica came into the room just then. "Don't worry, there's no one else here. Well, living at least."

We all relaxed a bit, then walked up into the main house. The windows being boarded up really helped with the whole privacy thing, and we didn't have to worry so much about being seen from the outside.

"Here, I'll show you where the body was found," I whispered, and led the girls through the various rooms of the ground floor.

We arrived at the end of the long corridor where I found Jessica's body, and I motioned to the doorway. "She was hanging here."

"Poor girl," Jane said quietly to herself.

Mr. and Mrs. Littleton appeared on the other side of the doorway, and Jessica joined them, standing directly under where her body was found.

"Okay," I said. "Now that you're here, do you remember anything else?"

She shook her head. Crap. Well, I knew it couldn't be that easy.

"Let's just wait a while, and hopefully, something will come to you," I said. "Close your eyes and relax, and try to think back to your very first memory as a ghost."

Jessica shut her eyes tight, and we all watched in silence while she tried to remember.

"I remember wandering around the house confused," she began. "I wasn't sure how I got here."

"That's good," I said. "Keep thinking. Was there anyone else in the house before we found you?"

She nodded. "Well, yeah, all the witches, and

that weird pale guy, but they were all part of the haunted house and came later. I was alone for a while before that."

"That's great Jessica, you're doing a good job," Jane said encouragingly.

She squeezed her eyes tighter, and we waited patiently.

"Was there anybody else here before that? Do you remember maybe even the smell or the sound of a person?" I asked.

A few moments passed and then she said, "Yes. I remember lots of cursing. It was a man's voice."

I smiled, she was remembering. "That's awesome. Now focus on that voice. Did he say anything else?"

She shook her head. "No, just swearing. I think he had trouble hanging up my body."

Jessica was a tiny girl, so that gave us at least some insight into her potential killer.

A creaking noise suddenly came from the next room, and we all froze in fear. I could feel my heart in my throat, and I cursed myself for not bringing some sort of weapon with us.

Rory reached for my hand and squeezed it with a death grip, but I was too focused on not peeing my pants that I hardly noticed.

Another creaking noise came from the room, sounding suspiciously like footsteps.

I swallowed hard and stepped in front of Rory,

not that I could have protected her without a weapon.

The footsteps grew louder, and I was paralyzed with fear. I did the only thing I could think of and braced myself to lunge forward to tackle whoever it was that was coming. I was absolutely not going to die that day, if I had anything to say about it.

A shadowy figure came walking around the corner, and I pounced, collapsing on him as he fell backward in a sloppy attempt at a tackle.

The figure screamed and pushed me off of it. I paused, and braced for an attack, but none came. A soft whimpering noise came from the shadowed figure.

I got my phone out of my pocket and held the light up against the person's face.

Ryan Bramley stared back at me.

"Ryan," I said, shocked. "What the hell are you doing here?"

The tension in the room eased slightly, and I heard Bailey let out a nervous giggle from behind me.

Ryan started up at me, his face as white as a ghost, his hands trembling.

I sat back and stared at him, waiting for an answer.

He stared up at me, terrified.

After a few long moments, he finally said, "I saw

you guys come in. I wanted to make sure you were alright."

"That's so sweet of you, Ryan," Bailey said from behind me. She walked up to us and reached her hand out to help him up. He refused it and pushed himself up off the floor.

I accepted her hand graciously, and she pulled me up to my feet to face Ryan.

"We could have killed you," I said.

"Yeah, with what weapon?" He tried to laugh, but it came out as an uncomfortable sounding wheeze.

The window creaked, and Ryan jumped.

"Don't worry, it's just the wind," I said.

"I should go," he said quickly. "This place isn't safe. You should all go, right now."

I nodded. "Yeah, you're probably right. You go on ahead; we'll catch up in a second."

Ryan then turned and ran out of the room, and we heard the slamming of the cellar door a moment later.

I turned to look at the girls, who looked back at me with expressions as shocked as mine was.

"Brave of him to come in here," Bailey said.

I rolled my eyes. "Brave of him to stay."

I shook out my arms to release the pent up tension I was holding, and let out a loud sigh. "Okay, let's get back to this."

Bailey suddenly froze, her eyes wide, staring into the room Ryan just ran off through.

"What?" I asked.

I noticed everyone else had frozen, too. What the hell?

I turned to see where they were looking and heard a soft click as I felt cold metal press against my temple.

My heart leaped into my throat again, and I felt my skin go ice cold. I turned my head as best I could with a barrel of a gun pressed to the side of my head, and found myself looking straight into the icy blue eyes of Jordan O'Riley.

CHAPTER NINETEEN

"What are you doing here?" Jordan growled, holding the gun steady against my head.

"You," I said breathlessly. "I knew it."

He dropped his gun hand away from me, pointing it to the floor instead. "What do you mean, you knew it?"

I shook my head. "This whole time. Why?"

He narrowed his eyes at me but didn't answer.

"I said, what are you all doing here?" he walked to the edge of the room, and we all stepped back away from him, our backs up against the far wall. He eyed us as we moved, but then proceeded to switch the light on.

"Please, don't hurt us," Rory said, falling to her knees. "Please, we didn't do anything, I swear."

"We won't tell anybody," Jane said.

I shushed them, then doing my best to act brave, I stepped forward towards the killer.

"I don't…" I began, but he cut me off before I could finish my sentence.

"Tell me why the hell you are all here," he growled again, looking back and forth between the four of us.

"We thought we could gain some insight about the killer," Bailey began reciting our cover non-story.

"And looks like we got what we came for," I said darkly, glaring at him.

He sighed. "Come with me."

"Please, we'll say nothing," Jane pleaded. "Just let us go."

"Come," Jordan growled and turned to leave.

I glanced back at the girls. "Don't think we have a choice in this."

I tried my best to remain calm, thinking of a way to get out of this situation. We didn't have weapons, but perhaps we could outsmart him.

I eyed Bailey behind me, and mouthed "Can you hex him?"

She shook her head. Her face had gone so pale she looked like she was about to faint.

I was surprised when he led us towards the front door and not down into the basement or someplace hidden.

He opened the door, then stepped to the side to

let us walk out.

I stepped cautiously, confused as to what was going on. I then saw Mayor Scott standing outside accompanied by Mrs. Brody, and then I was really confused.

"Come with me," the mayor barked, then stormed off towards his office less than a block away.

We all followed in silence, my heart beating very loudly in my chest. Jordan followed closely behind us, his gun still out.

As we all gathered in Mayor Scott's office, he slammed the door behind us and locked it. Jordan took a seat at the far side of the room.

"It's him," I shouted, pointing at Jordan. "He's the murderer. He came back to the scene of the crime, we saw him." I was shaking uncontrollably by this point and had to sit down to prevent myself from passing out. Mrs. Brody came to stand near me and put her hand on my shoulder. She kept her silence, though, and just watched the room from behind me.

Sheriff Reese then came walking into the office from the back room. "No, no he's not," he said coolly.

Mayor Scott sat in his chair, rubbing his temples. "Please, explain what you girls were all doing in the haunted house. I knew something was up when Mrs. Brody lured me back to my office." His eyes narrowed on her, and she stared daggers at him right back.

I took a few deep, calming breaths before I could speak. "I needed to go back into the house to see if I could get more information about the murder." I paused then, unsure as to what I should say in front of the sheriff. I looked at Mayor Scott and continued, "I had reason to believe there was untapped information to be found in the house."

He nodded, understanding what I was suggesting. "And did you find anything?"

I pointed at Jordan and nodded.

"Jordan is not the killer," Sheriff Reese repeated. "We're old buddies from the force. He's an undercover cop from Boston. We asked him to come up and help with the case."

I stared incredulously at Jordan. "You're a what?"

He shrugged. "Well it's not exactly like I could have told you that."

I shook my head. "I don't believe this. Why were you in the house then?"

"I heard a scream and came running. I flagged the mayor down on my way, so he knew I was going in there."

"Are you hurt?" the sheriff asked, looking us all up and down in turn. When he didn't notice any visible damage, he continued, "Why did you scream?"

"We didn't," I said. "Ryan did."

"Ryan Bramley?" Jordan asked.

I nodded. "Yeah, he was there just before you. Why?"

Jordan immediately stood up and ran out the back door.

I raised my eyebrow at Sheriff Reese who quickly said, "You should all leave. It's not safe here. Go home, I'll fill you all in tomorrow morning."

"Fat chance of that happening," I said. "What's going on, Sheriff?"

Not a few moments later, Jordan was dragging a handcuffed Ryan Bramley into the sheriff's office. Ryan was kicking and struggling, but Jordan was the stronger of the two.

"What the hell is going on, man?" He shouted, trying to squirm free of Jordan's grip. "Why the hell do you have handcuffs? What's going on?"

He quieted when he noticed we were all standing around the room watching him.

"It's them," he pointed a finger at Mrs. Brody. "They did it, I saw them. They're witches. They killed the kid and that old couple."

"Don't you point your scrawny little finger at me, you maggot," Mrs. Brody snapped at him. "You've always been a little weasel."

Jordan rolled his eyes. "Enough with the damn witches."

Ryan began to panic. "It wasn't me, I swear. I saw the old witch hang the girl up, I was just too scared to come forward because I thought she would curse me." He began struggling against the handcuffs again.

"Let him go," Bailey cried. "He's obviously incapable of this sort of thing."

"Shut up, witch," Ryan spat at her.

She stepped back in shock, her eyes brimming with tears. "Ryan?"

Realization slowly dawned on me. I stepped forwards towards the squirming boy before me. "You were going back to make sure you didn't drop anything."

He stared at me, wide-eyed.

"You got the idea after we were talking in the café, didn't you?"

Ryan gave up struggling and collapsed onto the floor, his eyes beginning to tear up.

"Why do you have to live with them?" he asked me. "I've told you so many times."

"What?" I looked around the room hoping for an explanation, but no one could offer anything to me. I stared back down at Ryan, waiting for him to continue.

"They're witches," he sobbed. "All of them. I was trying to protect you from them." He curled into a ball on the floor and continued to sob into his knees.

"I did it," he admitted. "It was me. I did it. But I did it for you."

I stepped back in disgust, and both Jordan and Sheriff Reese held their guns out, pointed at Ryan.

Ryan glanced up at Jordan. "What the hell dude? I thought we were friends?"

Jordan shook his head. "I'm not friends with monsters, man. How could you do that to those people?"

Ryan then began to sob even louder. "I didn't mean to kill her. I didn't mean to kill the kid. I just wanted to mark her. I just wanted to scare the town so they would chase out the witches." He took a few shuddering breaths, then continued. "She died, though, and then it was too late to go back."

"Why kill the couple?" Mayor Scott asked.

Ryan shook his head. "I'm not saying anything else. I want a lawyer."

Sheriff Reese sighed. "Alright then, Ryan. You'll get your lawyer. But for now, you're going to rot in prison."

The sheriff dragged Ryan kicking and screaming from the room, followed by Mayor Scott. Jordan stayed behind with us, his eyes focused on me.

I stared back at him, trying to make sense of the scene that just went down. The room was silent apart from Bailey's muffled sobs coming from behind me.

I stole a sympathetic glance in her direction, then turned back to Jordan.

"I'm sorry," I said to him.

"Don't be," he said. "You were acting on your gut instinct. It means I played my part well."

"How did you pull that off?" I asked, motioning towards the direction they took Ryan. Lights from the police car went by the front window, and I knew they were taking Ryan away to the local jail.

"I knew Ryan from Boston," he said. "We used to hang out. It was a good enough excuse to get me here without anyone questioning who I was."

"Did you have any idea?"

He shook his head. "None. To be honest, I was more concerned with his father, who often disappeared on weeknights. That was until I learned where he was going." He eyed Mrs. Brody but didn't say anything further.

"No," I said, my mouth falling open as I stared at Mrs. Brody.

"Oh, Mrs. Brody," Rory said. "Really? Mr. Bramley?"

She shrugged, a small smile forming on her lips. "Can't deny an old woman her simple pleasures."

I tried my best not to picture the two of them together. I had enough horror on my mind for one night, thank you very much.

I then thought of something. "The devil's root. Do you think Ryan stole it?"

Mrs. Brody nodded. "You can bet on it."

"That would also explain how he got through

your perimeter defenses," Rory said. "Because he'd already been in the house."

Jordan looked very confused with what we were saying but kept his mouth shut.

Mayor Scott came back into the room and sat down at his desk.

"Ryan's been taken to the station," he said. "He'll be sent to the state jail in the morning, and the feds will take over from there."

"I still don't understand why he killed the couple, though," Jordan said.

"I think I do," I answered darkly. "If he truly wanted to frame..." I paused, choosing my words carefully. "If he truly wanted to frame witches, then he had to make it look like the murders were going to continue to happen. I imagine whatever drug he used to paralyze them ended up being too much for Mr. and Mrs. Littleton to handle, and they died before he could mark them. But given his purpose of trying to frame the paranormal community, he had to put the marks on them anyway or else there would have been no point in killing them."

Mayor Scott nodded. "And he must have chosen those three because he somehow knew they were coming to Brimstone Bay. If they showed up with the markings…" He trailed off, lost in his thoughts.

"How did he know they were headed here?" Jordan asked.

I shrugged. "Facebook?"

"None of this explains the sewn lips," he continued.

"Maybe he didn't want the ghosts to blab about their killer?" I suggested, doing my best to sound innocent in the matter.

Mayor Scott looked up at me then, his eyebrows raised. "Then how?"

Jordan looked at him. "How what?"

I shrugged again. "I'd imagine ghosts probably wouldn't keep anything that happened to them after their bodies were already killed." I glanced back to Mrs. Brody, who nodded encouragingly to me. "But that's just a guess."

"You guys all sound mental," Jordan said. "What are you talking about?"

"You know, for a guy who grew up in a big city, you really don't seem to have a clue about any of this stuff," I said to him.

He shook his head. "I always figured it was just some sort of weird fetish people were into."

Rory then laughed. "Don't knock it 'till you try it."

I glared back and shushed her.

"This is all just a bit much for me," Jordan said, stretching and leaning back in his chair. "I've had enough crazy for one day."

Mayor Scott yawned. "Yeah, me too. I should go speak with Mr. Bramley, he'll need to be filled in on everything that happened."

I was going to wish him luck, but I really didn't know what to say. He was about to break the news to a sweet old man that his son was a murderer and would likely be locked away for the rest of his life. I felt terrible for the guy.

"Well, I think it's about time we all head home," Mrs. Brody chimed in.

"That's a good idea," Jordan said. "Would you ladies like a ride?"

"No thanks, we've got my car," Rory said.

We all got up to leave, and I turned back to Jordan. "I am sorry for suspecting you."

He shrugged. "It's no biggie. I would have done the same."

"Are you going to head back to Boston now?"

"Don't think so... I'll go see if I can do anything for the mayor and Mr. Bramley right now, then I'll stick around for a while and help wrap up the investigation."

I nodded. "Okay then, I'll see you around I guess?"

He smiled at me. "Definitely.'"

We all walked out of the mayor's office and stopped in the middle of the street to collect ourselves. Bailey had stopped crying, but I knew it would take a while for her to get over this.

I breathed in the cool autumn air, feeling somewhat invigorated after the events of the day. I looked around us, and the streets were peaceful. It had to be nearing morning by now, but the sky was still dark, and the lights were out in the shops. That is, apart from the mayor's office and one light down the road.

I sighed. "I should stop by the office on my way home. I think someone's still up there working."

"Want me to drop you off?" Rory asked.

I shook my head. "No thanks, I've still got my bike here."

My bike was still locked up to the street sign from earlier, and I waved goodbye to the girls and walked my bike back to the office. I could see through the window that JoAnn and Zack were still there. Likely stressing over the murder articles.

I leaned my bike up against the building and quietly made my way up the stairs. I pushed open the office door and was not prepared in the slightest for what I saw.

JoAnn and Zack pushed away from each other as I came in, both looking at me with wide-eyed and shocked expressions.

"Er, sorry," I muttered, totally embarrassed. Oh god, I can't believe they were just kissing. This better not mean Zack's staying in town.

JoAnn collected herself and brushed it off as if it were nothing, but Zack looked rather humiliated.

"I noticed the lights were on, and I thought I'd come fill you guys in on what happened," I said, feeling my cheeks grow warm as I spoke.

"What do you mean?" JoAnn asked. "What happened?"

"The murderer was caught," I said. "It was Ryan Bramley, from downstairs."

JoAnn looked absolutely shocked.

I filled them in on the story, then told Zack I was happy for him to finish the article. I really didn't have the emotional or physical capacity to work on this right now, and I really just needed to get home to bed.

JoAnn agreed that was a good idea, and we said our goodbyes. I could not get out of there fast enough.

I got back on my bike to head home and passed the storefront of the café. I saw Jordan and Mayor Scott standing in the middle of the room, and Mr. Bramley was sitting with his head on a table, hands covering his ears. I felt terrible for the poor guy and made a mental note that I would go back in a few days and offer to help out at the café. Or even better, I'll volunteer the services of my housemates. They really needed damn jobs.

The cool breeze felt good on my skin as I rode home, and I relished in the few minutes of silence I had to myself as I quietly rode my bike down the winding streets of town. After everything that had happened over the last few days, I was happy that it was now all over.

CHAPTER TWENTY

I SLEPT IN UNTIL LATE AFTERNOON THE NEXT DAY. I really must have needed the sleep, and my body was stiff when I woke up.

As if on cue, my trusty little furry companion pranced up to my face and curled into my pillow beside me. I nuzzled into his fur with my face, happy for the company. His purring comforted me as the memories of last night came back to me.

I was happy that the killer had been caught, but I was absolutely shocked that it was Ryan Bramley who did it. I hardly thought him capable of such a thing, and to think he did it to try and get rid of Mrs. Brody and my housemates. The thought made me sick to my stomach.

I then laughed silently to myself. I wondered what he would have done if he found out I was a witch, too. I mean, the signs were there, he was just too blind to see them.

I then thought of Bailey and resigned to push myself out of bed to go see how she was doing.

I was met in the halls with the smell of bacon and followed my nose down to Mrs. Brody's apartment.

The whole gang, including Jessica and Mr. and Mrs. Littleton, were clustered around the table, in a heated discussion about whether ghosts could smell bacon or not.

"Of course, we can," Mrs. Littleton was saying. "I can smell it now."

"You're a ghost, you have no senses," Mrs. Brody countered. "You're just imaging things."

"I can smell it," Jessica said. "I can almost taste it."

"Don't be ridiculous, girl," Mrs. Brody said, waving her hands at them dismissively. She then went back to cooking the bacon on the stove.

As per usual, Mr. Littleton just stood there silently, observing the scene around him. I wondered if he was this chatty when he was alive.

"Morning," I said as I joined them in the kitchen.

"Afternoon," Rory said back, smiling at me. "Have a good sleep?"

"You know it."

"I thought you could all use a nice hearty

breakfast," Mrs. Brody said to me as she poured me a cup of coffee.

"It's four o'clock," I laughed. "But breakfast sounds perfect."

We sat around the table, chatting happily over breakfast.

"What are you going to do now?" I asked Jessica and Mr. and Mrs. Littleton. "Your murders have been solved. Where will you go?"

Jessica looked sad. "I don't know."

"You'll come with us, of course," Mrs. Littleton said. "We've always wanted children, but never could have any of our own. We would love for you to stay with us. Isn't that right, dear?" She turned to look at Mr. Littleton.

Mr. Littleton looked at his wife with an expression of absolute happiness. He then turned to Jessica and said, "Oh yeah, I would love that very much."

I stared at him, surprised that he had finally spoken.

"Well that's lovely," Mrs. Brody said as she puttered about in the kitchen.

I noticed Bailey was quiet and not really eating. She was pushing her food around on her plate with her fork.

"You okay, Bailey?" I asked.

She nodded. "Yeah, fine."

"You know, there are plenty of other fish in the sea," Rory offered.

"Yeah, I know. It's not that. I just can't help but feel responsible for all of this."

"What?" I asked. "Don't be ridiculous. Bailey, this had absolutely nothing to do with you. Ryan was obviously sick in the head. Nothing any of us did could have caused this."

"I guess."

I sighed. The whole town was going to need time to recover from this, I imagined.

A knock came from the front door, and Mrs. Brody went to answer it.

"It's for you River, dear," she called back to me and winked at me as I passed her.

Jordan O'Riley was standing at the front door with two take-out coffees in his hands.

"Coffee?" he asked me.

I eyed him suspiciously but took a coffee from him. I opened the lid to peer inside. Black, just the way I like it.

I smiled at him. "Thanks, Jordan."

"Can we talk?" he asked.

I nodded. "Yeah, sure. Let's go around back."

I led him around the house to the back veranda, overlooking the bay. We probably had one of the nicest views in town.

"How are you doing?" he asked me. He looked

me up and down as if expecting to see some sort of physical damage.

"I'm fine," I assured him. "Just a little shaken up. I can't believe it was Ryan Bramley all along."

"Me neither," he said. "Trust me,"

"How do you guys know each other, again?"

"His mom lives just down the street from my parents. We hung out a lot as kids."

"You two really don't seem like you have a lot in common," I said, sipping my coffee.

"We don't. To be honest, I was surprised when he called me up last month when he was in town. He had come for some sort of gallery showing or something."

"Museum," I corrected him. "I think that's what started this whole thing. Did he know you were a cop?"

Jordan shook his head. "No, not many people do. I keep it quiet given the nature of my undercover work. I'm thinking of giving it up, though."

"Why is that?"

He shrugged. "It's not for me. I'd rather spend my days fishing, and you don't get much of that in the city."

"Just keep you fishing line to yourself," I said solemnly.

He nodded silently, and I could feel his eyes on me as I stared down into my coffee.

"Look, Mayor Scott filled me in on your guys', er…" He paused. "Nature."

I laughed. "He did, did he? And how did you react to that one?" Eyeing him, I tried to make sense of his facial expressions.

Jordan lifted his shoulder softly. "Took me a while to believe it, to be honest. But looking back at the things I've seen in Boston, it really doesn't surprise me that all that paranormal stuff actually exists."

"Wow, good for you," I said. "Most people refuse to believe it. There are only a few people in town who really accept it. The rest just think it's a made-up story."

He shrugged again. "I did too, for the longest time. So, can you actually do magic?"

A quick laugh spilled from my lips. "Some." I waved my hand in the air and muttered a few words under my breath. The early fall leaves in the back yard began swirling and lifted into a sort of fountain.

"Wow." His eyes sparkled as they followed the falling leaves. "That's amazing."

My lips twitched into a broader smile as I watched the amazement so plain on his face. "You're not afraid?"

Shaggy tendrils of sandy hair fell over his eyes as he shook his head. "Not in the slightest."

We both sat in silence for a few minutes, looking

out at the waves crashing in the bay, sipping our coffees next to each other.

"So, you really don't like pumpkin spice lattes?" he asked after a pause.

My laugh quickly turned into a cackle before I slammed my fist against my lips to suppress the sound. Biting my lower lip, I leaned over and nudged him with my shoulder as my smile grew. "I really don't like pumpkin spice lattes."

Milton Keynes UK
Ingram Content Group UK Ltd.
UKHW011310010324
438759UK00002B/298